Ghosts can't seem to keep their opinions to themselves.

Seventeen-year-old Nate Shaw should know; he's been talking to them since he was twelve. But they aren't the only ones making his high school years a living hell. All Nate wants is to keep his secret and keep his head down until he can graduate. That is, until the new boy, James Powell, takes a seat next to him in homeroom. James not only notices him, he manages to work his way into Nate's life. But James has issues of his own.

Between dead grandmothers and living aunts, Nate has to navigate the fact that he's falling in love with his only friend, all while getting advice from the most unusual places.

Ghosts, bullies, first love: it's a lot to deal with when you're just trying to survive senior year.

Copyright 2017 by Jennifer Cosgrove

Published by
NineStar Press
PO Box 91792
Albuquerque, New Mexico, 87199
www.ninestarpress.com

Print ISBN :1945952768
Cover by Natasha Snow
Edited by Elizabetta

A Boy Worth Knowing

Knowing

Jennifer Cosgrove

DEDICATION

Thank you.
To my husband, Stephen, for your love and support.
To my children. Love you always.
To Deborah, Melanie, and Amy for your cheerleading and general awesomeness.
To Jessica for pushing me down this crazy road to begin with.
And finally, to Gally, because everyone deserves a happy ending.

CHAPTER ONE

I loved autumn mornings.

The October air was just cold enough to set my lungs on fire, my breath visible in clouds of condensation, forcing all of the crap clogging up my head into the recycle bin. Bonus, I could pretend I was a dragon. Nothing could touch me; my morning run made everything go away, lost in miles at a time. Down an isolated country road.

Everything changed when I was twelve, and not for the better. That was when I started running. Five years of road I'd put behind me. My mom worried about me the first time I took off alone. Well, when she used to worry about me. I wished she was more worried about the reason I was running instead of the fact I was doing it down an empty road.

I turned the corner about a mile after leaving home, and that was when I saw him. Samuel was always lurking among the sunken headstones. Most people had no clue there used to be a cemetery out there. Looking closely, some of the stones that made up the foundation of the chapel could still be seen. No one else ever paid that much attention to it. Samuel glared at me as I got closer. He was a surly one.

My life was like the horror movies I loved. I talked to the dead. Well, technically dead. They were really spirits, or whatever. Whatever was left behind when people died. And they talked to me, for some reason. There was nothing like sitting in math class and having a ghost whisper in my ear while trying to take notes.

It happened all the damn time. I didn't know how to handle it at first. And no one wanted to hang out with the crazy kid in the back of the room, muttering away to himself. I got used to it. Really. And the lack of a social life helped me get all of my homework done on time; all of the teachers loved me. That was good. Talking to ghosts wasn't all bad.

I waved at Samuel as I ran by the cemetery. He shook a fist at me in return. Samuel wasn't evil or anything, just grumpy. Couldn't blame him, though. I looked him up one time and found out he'd died in the late eighteen hundreds. The cause of death on record was a heart attack.

But Samuel told me his brother-in-law had poisoned him because he wouldn't sell him his prize mule. I had no clue what was so special about that mule, but his brother-in-law evidently thought it was worth killing him over. I'd have been pretty surly myself.

Past the forgotten cemetery, a few miles to the McGregor farm, and then I'd swing around for home. Yes, I said McGregor farm. Small-town life— I couldn't have made this stuff up if I'd tried.

There was another house just past the farm where I had to watch out for their beast of a dog. Dogs weren't huge fans of mine. My Nana had a theory they could sense a bit of whatever it was that let us chat with those who'd "passed on." I had no idea how that was even possible, but cats loved me, so yay.

Speaking of which, Aunt Susan's overly fluffy cat waited by our mailbox. Arthur did that every time I went out for a run. He would sit there and then fall in behind to follow up the driveway until we got to the house. Then, it was a shady spot on the porch in the summer or, if it was cold like that day, into the house in front of the fireplace. I loved predictability.

The house used to be my grandmother's. It was a standard farmhouse, old and creaky just like dozens more all around us, and it could have stood a little paint. But we called it home, and we liked it. It became Aunt Susan's home. It had been left to her after Nana died, since my mom already owned one. It was a little out of the way and a long drive to the hospital where my aunt worked. But it was paid for, and that meant a lot.

I had to be quiet going in because Aunt Susan was not a morning person, and the floor squeaked just inside the back door. I was very much a morning person, and I followed the same routine each school or work day. Flipping on the coffee maker, I headed to my room to get ready for school. I got the shower running, since it took a while to heat up in an old farmhouse, and took a sniff to make sure a shower was actually necessary. Oh, yeah. I was gross.

I looked in the mirror like something was going to be drastically different from the last time I'd glanced at myself. Leaned into it to look at a pimple that was just starting to surface. Nice. Same brown eyes I shared with my mom and sister. Same pale skin that didn't tan so much as burn until I peeled and got a tiny bit of color. Same dark-brown hair that verged on unruly on a good day and untamable on a bad one. It was still all there.

* * *

The trouble started when I got out of the shower. There was nothing more frightening than walking to my room, minding my own business, and finding my Nana hanging out there. Especially since Nana had been gone for two years.

"Jesus Christ, Nana!" I grabbed my towel like it was going to make a break for it. I didn't care if she wasn't really there; I didn't want my Nana seeing my naked ass.

"Nathan Bernard Shaw, watch your language!" I cringed at the name. I was named after the playwright, not the journalist, by the way. He was my dad's favorite. At least, that was what Mom had told me years ago.

"Sorry." The towel was still trying to get away, and I tightened my death grip on it. "Um, can I have a few minutes?" Though dead, Nana Fran commanded respect. She'd been a tough lady when she was alive, but she'd understood me, and I missed her terribly. That didn't mean I wanted her in my bedroom while I was trying to get dressed.

"Of course, darling." Nana popped out of existence, and I shook my head to clear my ears. There had to be something of substance to ghosts or spirits because they always left a void when they went. I looked around just to make sure and then hurried to get ready.

* * *

Sure enough, just after I pulled on my T-shirt, Nana popped back in to perch on my desk chair. She'd always had impeccable timing. "Hey, Nana. What's new?"

She shook her head at me like she always did. "Smarty pants. How's school?"

"Fine." It was always fine.

"Grades good?"

"Yep. All good." They were always good.

"'Hanging out' with anyone new?" She even made air quotes.

Um. I never wanted to lie to Nana. I always felt guilty, and she always knew somehow. So I deflected. "Everyone's really busy right now. It's almost midterms, you know." Not a lie. Everyone was, in fact, busy with midterms.

She narrowed her eyes. I could literally see right through her, and she still made me flinch when she gave me that look. "When's the last time you had someone over?"

I pretended to think. It didn't take long because the answer was always never. "I'm not sure. A while?"

"A while." Nana gave me that look again, but I could tell she was going to let it go. That time. The next time, I might not be so lucky. "How's your mom?"

I made a face while she looked at me expectantly. I hadn't talked to my mother in almost a year. She lived only seven miles away, just past the McGregor farm and it had been that long. My mom was the reason I lived at Aunt Susan's, and not with her and my sister, Sarah. "Sarah says she's good."

"Sarah says, does she?" She was giving me that calculating look again. I ignored her in favor of digging socks out of a drawer. It was clear that tactic wasn't working when I heard her sigh. "Nate. Sweetie..."

"She doesn't want to talk to me, Nana." I hated the way saying it out loud made my chest hurt. A faint shimmer washed over her, which usually indicated a strong emotion. It was a mystery how it all worked, but a pissed off ghost glowed, and that was where she was headed.

"Has Susie tried to talk to her again?"

I didn't ask Aunt Susan to talk to my mom anymore. All it did was make her hurt and angry because then she had to tell me my mom didn't want to speak to me, and that made *me* hurt and angry. It was a vicious circle of suck. Deep breath. I would *not* cry before school.

"I stopped asking her to." I sat on the edge of the bed to put on my socks and to avoid eye contact. I was good at multitasking. "It just upsets her and then she wants to talk about it and then I just—" I squeezed my eyes shut to hold back the tears. *Not crying before school. Really.*

I felt a cold spot on my shoulder and knew if she were alive, Nana would be patting me there. "I know, sweetie. I don't understand her."

I didn't either. Edith Mae Shaw, formerly Bradley, was not able to deal with a son who could talk to the dead even though, technically, I'd gotten it from her. My grandmother had it, though not quite as strongly as me, and Aunt Susan had a touch of it. But my mom was a null when it came to ghosts and such. And what she couldn't see or understand made her afraid.

My unusual family situation usually required more of an explanation. My mom and dad, Edith and Robert, had worked great together. Until they didn't. My dad decided he wanted more things than our small town could offer, so he left. I was five and Sarah was three. Nana stepped in and helped. We stayed at her house more than at home until I was at least ten or so. Mom worked hard to support us. While my dad may have wanted more than a small-town life, my mom embraced it wholeheartedly. She went to church, joined the PTA, and did everything she thought she was supposed to do.

When I saw my first ghost, it changed how Mom treated me. I didn't realize what she was doing, of course; she never locked me in the basement or anything like that. The whole thing made her more and more uncomfortable. Over the years, it got to be too much, especially after Nana died. I wasn't stupid. I knew when I wasn't wanted.

I'd lost both parents and couldn't decide which one hurt more.

Aunt Susan had chosen me over her older sister, and I talked to my dead grandmother about all of my problems. It was something.

Nana always supported me—especially after my weird "gift" appeared. She was still supporting me even after cancer had stolen her away from us. I was getting a bit melancholy again. It happened.

I shrugged, and the chill from Nana's touch eased. "I don't want to talk about it right now. I've got to finish getting ready for school."

"All right, darling." She blinked back to the chair. "Talk to you later?"

I nodded and picked up my bag from where I'd thrown it the night before. "Sure. I'll tell you all about the grand adventures of Mountainview High School." I forced a smile. She gave me a worried look but didn't say anything before fading away. Heaving a sigh of relief, I checked the time on my phone. It would be time to go soon, and that meant making sure Aunt Susan was upright and functional to drive. She so wasn't a morning person.

I went back to the kitchen and put coffee in mugs—one with cream and sugar and one bitterly black. I set mine on the table and walked to Aunt Susan's bedroom door. Three knocks, and then the door opened just enough to admit the black coffee.

"Thirty minutes, okay?" I said into the gap. A grunt, and then I went back to my breakfast—coffee and frozen waffles fresh out of the toaster, the breakfast of champions. It worked.

I had just finished my third waffle when I heard shuffling feet behind me. "Ten minutes." A grunt and then a hair ruffle, so that was progress. I shook my head to try to bring the mop back under control as Aunt Susan sat at the table. "I talked to Nana earlier."

That got her attention. As I said, Aunt Susan had a touch of the "gift," but she couldn't see the dead; for her, it was more of a feeling than anything else. "What did she say?"

My coffee cup stared back at me as I looked into the bottom of it. "She wanted to know if I'd talked to Mom."

Aunt Susan snorted, and it made me smile. I might be young and stupid, but I knew what she'd done for me.

"Don't worry about it, Nate. She'll come around." That was Aunt Susan. She lived in perpetual hope things would work out, but she was always willing to accept that sometimes they just didn't. She was kind of awesome.

"I know."

She patted my arm, and it was time to go. Aunt Susan, a nurse, worked second shift at the local hospital, but she always took the time to drive me to school. I usually caught the bus home, which was another mark against me socially, but I couldn't be bothered to care. Nope. Not at all.

I had my license, but there was only Aunt Susan's Honda, so I dealt with it. She let me have it on the weekends, sometimes, but I didn't really ever do anything. There was one movie theater in town that had a classic movie weekend once a month, and I'd check that out. I loved old slasher films with a passion.

* * *

The route to school took us past Samuel, standing alone in the field in his burial suit. I waved at him as we drove by, and he made another rude gesture. Aunt Susan saw me out of the corner of her eye and grinned.

"Still surly?" She couldn't see him but always listened when I talked about the things I saw and heard.

"Oh, yeah. He's flipped me off twice already." I settled into the seat for the half-hour ride to school. It was usual for living out in the sticks, and it took longer on the bus.

"Did Coach Morgan talk to you about track again?" Aunt Susan wasn't going to let it go. She thought I should join the track team because it would help me "make friends and it looks good on a college application." I tried not to roll my eyes too hard. I didn't want to strain anything.

"Nope. I managed to avoid him." He'd been after me to join up since he drove by and saw me running a week ago. The man was persistent. Personally, I thought it was because our track team sucked, and he was desperate. It was her turn to roll her eyes.

"Nate"—exasperation dripped from her words—"I really think you should give it a try. You've got the perfect build for track and, you never know, you might make some friends. Have something in common with someone." Aunt Susan could also be a little delusional.

I smiled at her. "Why on earth would I want to do that?" She smacked me on the arm and turned her attention back to the road.

* * *

Mountainview High was the quintessential boring Midwestern high school. It was old, it smelled funny, and it was full of teenagers. Which was probably why it smelled funny. I shrugged on my backpack, held my head high, and walked right past the snickering group of cheerleaders just inside the door. They didn't like me because the boss of them, Penny Applegate, had caught me talking to Carl, who was the school janitor back in the nineteen fifties. He really liked it here for some reason. Penny had started calling me "Crazy Nate" because she was so *creative*, and it caught on with her minions.

I hated them.

The only thing keeping me sane was the fact I was graduating and would be getting the hell out of this place in a few months. It was more like eight, but who was counting? I'd be moving on to bigger and better things. At college, people wouldn't know anything about me, and I wouldn't be "Crazy Nate" anymore.

I nodded to Carl as he ghost mopped the floor. I couldn't explain that either. I didn't know if that was something they did out of habit, but it was always a little unnerving. There seemed to be rules regarding ghosts, but I'd only been able to figure out a few of them.

First and foremost was that recent deaths had an unpredictable and overwhelming effect on me. Those could be pretty unsettling, especially if the departed hadn't realized they were dead. Not long after I'd gotten my license, I'd driven past a horrible car accident and had seen the ghost of a young woman screaming by the mangled car—just one continuous scream. I usually didn't sleep well as it was, but that had kept me up for several nights in a row.

My second rule was that ghosts tended to stick, for lack of a better word, to people or places that meant something to them. That was why good ol' Carl hung out at school and why Samuel stayed in his graveyard. Carl loved the school and got to continue caring for it for as long as he wanted. Samuel was just angry that his brother-in-law was buried in the same place as him. I guess it made sense to him.

Everything else, I was making up as I went along. Nana told me a few things, but she always said that I'd just have to figure some stuff out on my own. It'd worked so far.

The bell rang, the cue for homeroom. Another school day. Yay.

CHAPTER TWO

Homeroom was...not terrible. Penny Applegate and her minions aside, everyone pretty much left me alone. Except for Mr. Gardener. I had made the mistake of asking him about something I saw in a science documentary, and he decided he needed to mentor me. I honestly couldn't remember what I'd asked him about so that I could make sure to never do it again. I mean, he was nice enough and all, but I could only make polite conversation about the decline of honeybees for so long. *I'm only human.*

He gave me a big smile, but I hurried to my seat seconds before the bell rang. I was in the process of getting my notebook out to look over my calculus notes one more time when I heard a commotion at the front of the classroom. I looked up just as the school secretary walked in with someone I'd never seen before.

He had his head down, but I could tell he wore glasses, even though his blond hair was hanging over them, hiding his eyes. His hair did that *thing* that not enough product in the world could make mine do. He looked up and scanned the classroom.

Oh. Oh no.

I ducked my head so we wouldn't make eye contact and tried to control what my face was doing. Pale skin meant everyone knew when I was embarrassed, and my cheeks had already started to heat. He was hot—as in, really good-looking. Mr. Gardener was talking, but I wasn't paying attention. Until I heard my name. *Damn.*

"Nate?" I glanced up to find Mr. Gardener looking at me expectantly and, for some reason, Penny was staring daggers at me.

"Sorry. What?" I was an idiot, and Blondie was grinning at me. My face was on fire.

Mr. Gardener gave me a forgiving smile. "I said, would you mind showing Mr. Powell here around?"

Oh my god, why did the world hate me? *No. Say no.*

"Sure." *Moron.*

"Splendid. James, go have a seat by Nate, and he'll take care of you."

Take care of him... I didn't think my face could get any redder, but apparently, I was wrong. *Calm down, Shaw, deep breaths help*. The new kid took the seat next to me and put his bag on the floor.

"Hey."

Oh hell. He had a nice voice, too. *Say something*.

"Hi." Whew!

"James Powell." He was actually holding out a hand to shake. *Oh my god*.

I managed to shake his hand without passing out. "Nate Shaw. Um, Nathan, really, but everyone calls me Nate." *Stop talking, you idiot!*

James smiled. "Nice to meet you, Nate." I nodded vaguely and pretended my calc notes were just that interesting. He was still watching me, and I turned to look into bright blue eyes. "Mind if I show you my schedule?" When I nodded, he grinned again like I'd just done something clever.

I was going to die before the day was over.

* * *

It turned out James and I had two classes and lunch together. Mr. Gardener let us out a few minutes early so I could show him around. We were walking down the main hall when I saw it.

It was just a flicker, but it was there—like a horror movie where the ghost suddenly appeared behind the hero and scared the crap out of everyone. That was kind of what the flicker looked like, except it sort of faded in and out. One second it was there, and the next it wasn't.

James, Mr. Nice Smile, had a spirit clinging to him.

As if things weren't weird enough.

I kept my eyes forward and tried not to pay attention to it. Experience had taught me that if I did, it would notice and interact with me, and I'd like to at least make it to lunch before James ran screaming. We had plenty of time for that. Speaking of which, once I got past the "Oh dear god, this beautiful human being is talking to me" thing, James seemed like a genuinely nice guy. Not that it'd matter once Penny got her claws into him, but it was nice to pretend. Oh, well.

"And that's the media center." I waved at our sad excuse for a library in true dramatic fashion. It made James smile again, so it was worth it. "I think that's it. If anyone tries to tell you there's a pool on the roof, don't believe them." That got a laugh.

"I'll keep that in mind." The bell rang, and he looked at his schedule again. "So 104 is that way?" He pointed in the right direction.

"Yep. See you around?"

"Sure." He moved to leave and then suddenly turned back. "Hey, Nate?"

I was still standing in front of the media center like an idiot, totally *not* watching him walk away. "Yeah?"

"Thanks." He gave me a smile and walked off. My cheeks heated again. I needed to work on my poker face if I didn't want to embarrass myself in some horrifying way before the day was over. What was I *doing*?

The bell rang again.

Dammit.

* * *

I made it to Calculus seconds after the last bell stopped ringing. *What is there to say? I'm fast.* Mrs. Robinson was not impressed.

"So glad you could join us, Mr. Shaw." She always did that. It was annoying and condescending. She probably didn't mean it that way, but that was how it came across.

"Sorry, Mrs. Robinson." I took my seat near the back and pulled out my book. It could have been written in Sanskrit for all I cared because I wasn't paying the least little bit of attention to it. All I could see were those eyes and that smile. I needed to get a grip. It was useless fixating on that kind of crap. I mean, it was only a matter of time before the cretins filled him in on what they thought of me. He seemed friendly, but that wouldn't last.

Sigh. Back to Calculus. At least in math, there was always a correct answer.

* * *

My resolve not to think about James and his perfect hair lasted until lunch. It wasn't my fault, though; it was his. I was sitting alone in the back corner of the cafeteria at my usual table when he plopped his tray down and sat with me like it was nothing. It startled me so much I almost knocked over my chocolate milk.

"Sorry! I didn't mean to scare you." James pushed his glasses up his nose and looked at me from under that flop of blond hair. I very cleverly wiped the chocolate milk from where it had sloshed on my wrist. *Smooth, that's me.*

"It's fine. I was almost done anyway." I pushed the tray with its disappointing excuse for a ham sandwich away. "How're you liking it so far?"

James poked at what passed for meatloaf and then put his fork down. "It's okay, I guess. Just new, you know?"

No, I didn't know. I'd lived here my entire life, and nothing was ever new. *Until now.* "Yeah. Um, where did you move from?" I immediately regretted asking because he gave me that look—the one where someone tried to smile and acted like it was nothing when it was obviously something they didn't want to talk about. To make matters worse, the spirit I'd been ignoring decided to make an appearance just behind him. I focused on the table because staring at James like a crazy person wasn't an option. "Sorry. If you don't want to—"

He shook his head. "No, it's fine." He poked at the meatloaf again. "We moved from Cincinnati to be closer to family. It was kind of sudden."

The spirit flared a little brighter, but I didn't let it distract me. *What could I say in these kinds of situations?* "Oh. Sorry." It was lame, but I was sorry he seemed upset by the whole thing.

"It's fine." He blew out a breath and pushed his glasses up again. Blue eyes met mine, and there was a jolt of connection. Blink. *Breathe.* I was about to say something completely awkward but was saved from myself by the appearance of Penny and her flunkies at our table.

Oh god, here we go.

"Hi, James." Penny's saccharine-sweet voice made my teeth hurt. To James's credit, he did look kind of annoyed at the interruption. It made me like him even more.

"Hello. Penny, was it?" He gave her a small smile, but I could tell he was being polite. Penny didn't bother looking at me. I didn't exist on her planet, much less in the cafeteria.

"Oh, you remembered! How sweet!"

I couldn't stand her. Her and her flippy hair. And stuff. She was pretty; I'd give her that. I could appreciate something beautiful, even when it was rotting inside. She had great hair and a great body, but it still didn't save her from being an awful person. I didn't think anything could do that. Oh god, she was still talking.

"Why don't you come and sit at our table so we can get to know you better?"

There it was. The invitation to the popular club. It had been fun while it lasted.

"No thanks, I'm good."

James was still giving her that polite smile and, more importantly, he wasn't getting up. Why wasn't he getting up? *Oh, now Penny gives me her attention.* If looks could kill.

"Really? Because all I see here is a crazy freak. Trust me, you don't want to get too close, it might be catching."

I tried not to react, really, but it still stung even when the person lashing out was an idiot. I drew up my shoulders defensively and forced myself to sit up straight, but it was too late, he'd already seen it. I saw confusion in his eyes and decided I'd make it easy for him.

"I'm done. I'll see you later?" I didn't wait for an answer, just dumped my tray and left. The library was always a good place to hide.

* * *

I didn't see James again until PE. I generally liked PE because the physical activity didn't leave many opportunities for people to talk or interact with me in any way—unless it was basketball or something. Hey, getting picked last for a team even though I was a decent player felt great! *Yeah, it really didn't.* Plus, any chance of physical contact allowed them to exploit it. Not anything over the top, but I'd had my nose bloodied more times than I could count by an "accidental" elbow. The nurse and I were good pals.

That day, there was a fitness test, so out to the track we went. At least it was something I could do alone. Running laps pushed what had happened at lunch out of my head and helped me forget about everything else for a while. I had barely registered the pounding footsteps before James caught up with me.

"What happened to you?" he said, breathing hard from sprinting. I ignored the question for a minute or two, listening to the sound of our feet on the track instead. It was an odd sound. I always ran alone; hell, I did everything alone. And since he'd caught his breath and was waiting for an answer I didn't want to give. He moved a little closer and lowered his voice. "Penny's a bit of a bitch."

I couldn't help it. The bark of laughter came out of nowhere; it felt kind of wonderful. When Coach Morgan glanced at us, I did my best to control my face before he said something. I also kept my voice low so we wouldn't attract any more attention. "Yeah. It's kind of her thing."

"What's her problem?" James sounded genuinely curious. It made me wonder if he'd ever had anyone in his life who hated him just for existing. I couldn't imagine he had. "I mean, specifically with you?"

"Specifically? She just doesn't like me." I put my head down and sped up, just a bit, but James was meeting me stride for stride. He must run as well. Or something. "Fine. She hasn't liked me since we started high school. She thinks I'm 'weird.'"

"Oh." We ran in silence for a few more minutes. Only one lap to go, and this awkward conversation could be forgotten forever. "There's someone like that in every school. And because there's someone like that in every school, there's always someone like you."

I stumbled and almost crashed, right there on the track. I got it together and kept going. "And what does that mean?"

James looked at me sideways. "It means you're worth knowing." He lengthened his stride and left me behind. I could only stare at his back in wonder.

* * *

Back in the locker room, I was still thinking about that odd conversation. I didn't shower because that was just asking for trouble. All the way through Spanish, I thought about it. I still hadn't figured James out by the time I got to World Lit, but I had to put it aside because he was sitting right there. In the seat next to mine. I froze in the doorway and had to make myself move to get out of the way. How did he know?

Of course. No one ever sat next to me, and Mrs. Grady must have pointed him toward the empty seat. *Okay. Don't make this awkward.* I put my backpack on the floor next to my desk and very casually dropped into my seat. So casually that the whole damn thing slid a few inches, making the loudest screeching sound that ever existed. So I did what anyone else would; I looked around in confusion to see where the sound had come from because it certainly hadn't come from my desk. Nope.

I glanced over at James, and he had a tiny smirk on his face. On anyone else, I would have assumed it was mocking and expect to be embarrassed. Loudly. But somehow that wasn't the case. I allowed myself a smile as I retrieved my notebook and textbook from my bag. When I straightened up, he'd turned to look at me, his chin propped in his hand. His glasses sat crookedly on his nose, and it was all I could do not to stare.

"Very smooth, Nate." He was grinning widely at me. What was it like to be able to do that? I looked at my notes and tried not to blush.

"Shut it."

He chuckled, and I was quietly overwhelmed by the idea that someone wanted to talk to me.

* * *

I hated riding the bus. As a senior, it was akin to social suicide, something to be stared at and mocked mercilessly about. Unfortunately, I had no choice. Aunt Susan's work schedule and our lack of a second car left me with very few options. I had walked home before, and I'm sure I would again.

The only good thing about taking the bus was that I got to see my little sister, Sarah. We went to the same school and lived just a few miles apart, but the only time we got to talk was on the bus. I couldn't decide if that was sad or just painful. It was probably a bit of both.

I was one of those rare older kids who truly liked their younger sibling. Sarah was awesome and, despite her relation to me, fairly popular at school. We shared Mom's dark curly hair, but while mine was unruly, hers looked like she actually knew what to do with it. I tried not to hold it against her. I was staring out the window when she dropped into the seat next to me.

"Greetings, big bro!"

"Greetings." She waved at someone in the back of the bus, smiling the entire time. Oh, to be fifteen and loved by the world. Did that make me sound ancient? She knew what I was, knew why I'd left, and she was still accepted by our mother. She also had a touch of what I had but made sure to hide it down deep. The only time it was ever mentioned was when it was just the two of us.

She nodded at the window. "What's he doing this time?" Sarah couldn't see Samuel, but I'd told her about him, and she could feel him somehow. I glanced out the window and laughed.

"He's naked." She wrinkled her nose at me, and I looked again. "Okay, you don't want to know what he's doing now."

She smacked me on the shoulder. "You're gross."

I raised my hands in protest. "Hey, I didn't do it." We both broke into giggles that felt so good. I missed her so much. The thought was enough to drive my smile away. "Um, how's Mom?"

Her face fell, and she looked away. "Nate…"

"Sorry." I wished I could delete the words and go back to silly giggles. We both hated the whole situation, but there wasn't anything to be done about it until Mom came to her senses. Or I went away to college. Whichever came first.

Sarah blew out a breath. "It's fine. She's fine. She got that promotion she was so excited about."

"Good. That's good." *Ugh, so awkward. Time to change the subject.* "So, how are things with Charlie?" That got her. Her face turned red, and she smacked me on the arm again.

"*Shut up!*" She looked toward the back of the bus at the dark-haired boy who was currently talking, very expressively, to his friend. "You suck."

"That well, huh." I couldn't help it. She'd had a crush on Charlie Monroe since they were ten. I'd caught him looking at her too, so it seemed like the feeling was mutual. Not that she would ever have taken my word for it.

"You are the worst brother ever." She tried to look mad, but I could see the grin trying to get out. She looked out the window. "Oh, thank god. Here's my stop." She grabbed her backpack and stood as the bus slowed. "See you around, big bro." Sarah ruffled my hair and darted away when I tried to swat her hand. I waved as she walked down the steps and watched as she checked the mailbox before walking down the driveway to the house where I used to live.

God, I missed her.

Chapter Three

Arthur was waiting for me when I got to Aunt Susan's house. I still had a hard time calling it home no matter what it said on all of my school forms. His Fluffiness stretched up to demand ear scratches as I checked the mail—junk and bills. I doled out the required scratches, and Arthur followed me into the house.

Open the fridge for a snack and then homework. Yes, I really am that boring. If I got it done, I could basically do whatever I wanted. Aunt Susan ran a tight ship, but it was a pirate ship. There were "guidelines." The main one was: do well in school and you'll be free to do anything legal your little heart desires. It was a good guideline, and I hadn't gone against it up to that point. *What can I say? I'm a bit of a nerd.*

I was working my way through the *Hamlet* reading for World Lit when my phone pinged at me. A glance at the screen showed it was an email notification. Which was weird because it was from a student account. No one ever emailed me from school. Ever.

I slid a finger across the screen to look at it and almost dropped my phone. It was from James. *Oh god.* I blinked at the screen and swallowed. It was ridiculous; I most certainly was not crushing on him. I'd only just met him, for Christ's sake! And he was...nice. To me.

I took a deep breath and opened up the email.

To: nshaw@mountainviewhs.edu
From: jpowell@mountainviewhs.edu

I figured out your school email. I hope you don't mind. I've got a question about the chemistry homework. Can you help?
James

He wanted my help with homework. Mine. Why me? I put the phone down carefully and paced around the kitchen. I picked it up again to make sure the email was still there. It was. I put it back on the table and looped around the kitchen. Arthur jumped down from the windowsill and followed me for a few passes around the table. He finally got bored with my drama and curled up on one of the chairs.

I froze. Read receipt. All school emails automatically sent a read receipt. How long had it been since I'd opened the email? Did he think I was ignoring him? *Calm down*. It'd only been a few minutes. I tapped out a reply.

To: jpowell@mountainviewhs.edu
From: nshaw@mountainviewhs.edu

Sure.
Nate.

Smooth. Very smooth. I was berating myself for being an idiot when another email came in.

To: nshaw@mountainviewhs.edu
From: jpowell@mountainviewhs.edu

Great! Can I call you?
James

Oh.

What was I supposed to do? I squeezed my eyes shut and tried to remember I was a reasonably intelligent person who did not fall apart over talking to someone on the phone. Even if that someone was a very good-looking guy who wanted to talk to me. About Chemistry. Stick to the homework, and it'd all be okay. I could do this.

I opened my eyes and hit reply, responding with my phone number and some inane thing about being happy to help. My finger hovered over send for a few moments of self-doubt, and I jabbed it before I could change my mind or make myself look stupid.

I put the phone facedown on the table and tried to concentrate on *Hamlet* again, but it rang after just a few minutes. I let "Enter Sandman" play for a few seconds so I wouldn't look too eager, and answered.

"Hello?" I pulled a face. I always sounded dumb answering the phone. I'd much rather text.

"Hey, Nate. It's James." I was about to reply when he continued, "Sorry, but I missed the homework assignment in Chemistry. Did you write it down?"

I nodded, realized he couldn't see me, and wanted to bang my head against something. Why was I so freaking awkward? "Yeah. Hang on, let me get my notebook." I rummaged around in my backpack. Of course I couldn't find it. I was holding the phone between my ear and shoulder, digging with both hands when James started to talk again.

"It's okay if you don't have it. I can always play the 'I'm the new kid and don't know what I'm doing' card." I laughed and finally found the elusive notebook.

"Got it!" I flipped through the pages for a moment. "I'd save that card for something other than chemistry homework. Mr. Gardener is a pushover." James chuckled, and something fluttered in my stomach. *Stop it.* I read off the assignment and tried not to stutter.

"Thanks. So, what's there to do around here?" I didn't know what to say. I guess I expected him to hang up since I'd served my purpose.

"Um." *Yeah. Fantastic.* "There's the movie theater."

"I saw that. Looks like they're doing a movie marathon this weekend." I knew that. I knew that because I'd already asked Aunt Susan if I could use the car on Saturday.

"Yeah. Kubrick. I was going to go." I could almost hear him smiling. What was going on?

"I love Kubrick! Want some company?"

Oh god. He wanted to go with me. Wanted to go *with* me. *Say something, stupid!*

I cleared my throat. "Sure. I was going to borrow my aunt's car—"

"Oh, don't worry about that. I can drive." I could hear him shifting the phone around and someone talking in the background. "We'll talk about it later. My mom just got home, and I've got to help her with the groceries."

We said our good-byes and hung up. I put the phone down on the table and leaned hard on the edge. What had I just agreed to? Was it a date? No. Not a date. Didn't want to even think that. God, I needed to talk to *someone.*

I grabbed my book and wandered into the living room. Flopping down on the couch didn't help anything. Neither did staring at the ceiling.

"What has you all tied up in knots?"

I nearly fell off the couch. "Holy shit!"

"Language, young man!" Nana looked at me sternly from the rocking chair in the corner. It was worn smooth from years of use and rocked slightly as if in a breeze. I wasn't sure how it worked. It just did.

"Sorry. You startled me." I gave her a smile. "Again."

"You were in your own little world. Again." She smiled and leaned back in the chair, folding her hands in her lap. "What's going on, darling?"

I didn't know how to say it. She'd always had the impression I did normal things, like have friends and hang out. I'd never done that. Not much since I was twelve when this *thing* had started, and certainly not since I'd started high school. "Um, I think I might have a friend."

"A friend?" She absolutely beamed at me. "That's wonderful, darling!" She winked out of the rocking chair to stand next to the couch. She moved her hand as if she was going to pat my shoulder but stopped herself. "Why the face?"

"What face?" I tried to smile but must have looked confused. Nana pursed her lips, which meant she wasn't buying it. At all. I went back to studying the ceiling. "I don't know."

There was no movement to the couch cushion when she sat down next to me. That kind of thing had been a little disconcerting at first, but I had gotten used to it. She leaned a little closer, concerned. "What happened?"

Great. Now I have to talk about it. To my Nana. Embarrassing. "There's a new kid at school." I rolled my head over to look at her and sighed. "His name is James." She nodded and waited for me to go on. Nana always was easy to talk to. I looked back up, once again engrossed in the ceiling. "He's nice."

I could practically feel the smirk. "He's nice? As in, nice-looking?" My face heated. *Dammit.* Yes, Nana knew. No, she didn't have a problem with it. "Are we talking about a little crush on the new boy?"

Crush. I winced at the word. It seemed so juvenile. I was seventeen years old. That was practically an adult. I didn't get crushes. Did I? *Oh god.* That stupid fluttering in my stomach was back. "I don't know." That was becoming my mantra apparently. "I just met him," I reminded her. "Isn't that a little soon for a crush?" Blech. I hated that word.

"Not necessarily. I knew I was going to marry your granddad after knowing him for only a day." Nana leaned in, taking over my view of the ceiling. "It's not that unusual."

I ignored the word "marry." *No. Just no. Sigh.* "I can't tell if he even, you know."

"Likes you?" She always did get right to the point.

"Likes boys." That was the question. He wanted to go to the movies with me. What if it was a date? What if it wasn't? What if I thought it was, but it wasn't? I was a mess.

"You're a mess." I hated when she did that. She was still blocking my view, but she was cheating. Floating was cheating. "Nate, darling, let me give you some advice." I raised my head, and she settled back onto the couch. When she put her hand on my knee, the goosebumps rose there, under the shade of her fingers. "Be his friend."

I raised my eyebrows at her. She made everything seem so simple. "Be his friend?"

"If you can be his friend first, everything else will either fall into place"—she put her hand on my cheek, and the hairs on the back of my neck stood up in protest—"or it won't. Just try not to worry about everything along the way, okay?"

She narrowed her eyes when I nodded. She would have pinched my cheek if she could. "Yes, Nana." And that was that. She blew me a kiss before she faded away. I did feel better. At least I wasn't working myself up into a panic anymore. I picked up *Hamlet* and tried to find my way back to Denmark again.

* * *

The next day started the same way they all did. I went on a run, got insulted by Samuel, said hi to Arthur, got ready for school, and delivered coffee to Aunt Susan. At school, I managed to duck past Penny and her cohorts unscathed before finally making it to homeroom. It was a relief not having to deal with the comments. James wasn't there yet, but I tried to push it out of my mind and concentrate on my calculus notes for first period. I was evidently doing a good job of it because I jumped about a foot when James dropped into the seat next to me.

"Sorry." He grinned at me, his eyes sparkling behind his glasses. *Sparkling? I have to get a grip on myself.* Okay, bad choice of words. "Thanks for your help last night."

"Anytime." See? Easy. I could totally do this. I caught Penny's glare out of the corner of my eye. She needed to get over herself.

"What time does the first movie start on Saturday?" He still wanted to go. To the movies. With me. *I couldn't do this.*

"I think *Dr. Strangelove* starts at two." There were three movies. That meant approximately seven hours of time in a darkened theater. *Breathe.*

"Text me your address, and I'll pick you up around one or so." I nodded and dutifully tapped out my address. He looked it over. "That's not too far away from my house."

I blinked at him. Not that many people lived out my way. "Really? Where do you live?"

"You know Sam McGregor?" I nodded because I did indeed know Sam McGregor. He and Aunt Susan had dated for a little while. They broke up a while back but were still friends. I thought she still missed him, though. "He's my mom's brother." James fidgeted with his phone and looked away. "We're living with him for a while."

"Oh. Well that's, um." I wanted to ask so many questions, but it was obvious he was uncomfortable talking about it. The little bits and pieces were starting to come together. Luckily, for both of us I think, the bell rang and saved us from our combined awkwardness.

"See you at lunch?" He looked at me expectantly, and I did the only thing I could.

"Sure. See you there."

* * *

Lunch was...good. It was great talking to someone instead of hiding in the library or dodging insults from the popular crowd. In addition to Kubrick movies, James also liked classic horror movies and Metallica, among other things. It was amazing. It was so amazing I almost forgot about the spirit hanging on to him. Until I made the mistake of looking at it.

The bell had just rung, and we were gathering our things to go when I let my guard down. Luckily, James hadn't been looking at me, because that would have ended things right then and there. It was when I looked up that it locked eyes with me. Remember that weird flicker thing I said spirits did? It jumped from him to me in a heartbeat, nose an inch away from mine. It was all I could do not to react. I turned my head and whispered "Later" at it. Sometimes, that worked. The promise of acknowledgment was sometimes enough to momentarily satisfy the need for my attention. It looked at me closely, flickered back to James, and I could breathe again.

James turned around and caught me staring. I glanced at the clock and hurried to grab my bag before he could say anything. "Uh-oh. See you in PE?" He nodded, and I took off in the direction of my next class. I was going to have to deal with that spirit eventually.

Because I knew who it was. It had to be a close relative—maybe a brother? They had the same eyes.

CHAPTER FOUR

The next few days passed by slowly. The movie marathon thing both excited and filled me with dread. I referred to it as "thing" because I still hadn't quite figured out what it was. Were we just hanging out? Yes. That was exactly what we were going to be doing. I was going to take Nana's advice and just go with it.

Aunt Susan asked me about my Saturday plans as she drove me to school on Friday. "You'll need the car. Or did you want me to drop you off?"

"Um. I'm going with James, and he offered to drive." I kept my eyes straight ahead but sensed her staring at me. She jerked her attention back to the road before I had to say something about it.

"James? Who's that?" She was trying to stay casual.

"He's, um, new." I felt the eye roll. "He's Sam's nephew."

"Oh." We rode in silence for a minute or two. "He'd mentioned his sister and her family were coming, but that was the last I heard of it. I just assumed they were visiting." Silence again. "What's he like?"

My face flushed. What the hell was wrong with me? "He's, um, he's nice."

"Nice?" She couldn't help but be skeptical. I hadn't specifically talked with her about all of the stuff that happened at school, but Aunt Susan was no dummy. She could figure it out. "Nate, are you sure?"

I nodded. I wanted to tell her it wasn't like the time I'd gotten an invitation to a birthday party only to find out later the date had been changed on my invite. I'd sat alone at the local skating rink for hours. It wasn't Mom's fault. I'd asked her to drop me off and go because I was trying to be cool.

It was awful.

So I couldn't blame Aunt Susan for a little overprotectiveness. "It's fine. He sits with me at lunch, and we have a few classes together."

She was still giving me the side-eye as if she didn't quite believe me. "Okay. If you're sure."

"I'm sure." And I was. Pretty much. Mostly. *I guess we'll see on Saturday.* "So, do you know anything about why they moved out here?" I was prying, but I really wanted to know what I was dealing with as far as the spirit that was following James around.

I could tell she knew something, too.

"Oh, Nate, I don't think I should say."

"Someone died, didn't they?" I was fishing; maybe she'd bite.

She shook her head. "I'm sorry." Her lips pressed into a tight line, and I figured I was right.

"Okay." I dropped it, but I couldn't stop thinking about it.

* * *

Saturday arrived as if everything was normal and right with the world. I was a nervous wreck and couldn't put my finger on why that was. To help, I went for a run though I usually took Saturday off. Muscles had to rest. It was my sleep-in day, but that just wasn't going to happen.

When I got home, Aunt Susan wasn't up yet, of course. She didn't have to go in to work and would probably sleep until noon. Coffee and breakfast for one it was. Unless I counted the bacon I shared with Arthur. It totally counted.

I got dressed and then looked at the time. It was only nine o'clock. How was it only nine o'clock? I slumped onto the couch and looked around. What could I possibly do for four more hours? Arthur jumped up and made himself at home on the cushion next to me. I buried my fingers in his fur and gave him a good scratch.

"So what now, Arthur?" He purred at me. "Yeah, I know. Waiting sucks."

* * *

I got through two and a half episodes of *Doctor Who* before Aunt Susan made her way into the land of the living. I pointed to the kitchen where the coffee was just finishing up. She fixed a cup and joined me on the couch on the other side of Arthur. We watched the Doctor deal with the Weeping Angels, and I turned it off.

"What time is James picking you up?" I should've known I wouldn't get out without more questions.

"Around one." She nodded, and I could tell she wanted to say more. "What?"

She shrugged and took another sip of coffee. "Just curious." I turned to look at her, eyebrows raised. Shaking her head, she put her mug down with a *clink*. "Okay, fine. I'm just worried."

That didn't surprise me, but I played along. "Why are you worried?"

She looked away, frowning. "I just— I don't want you to get hurt."

"Get hurt? We're just going to see a few movies." At least that was what I'd been telling myself for the past few days. I couldn't deny the churning in the pit of my stomach and chalked it up to spending leisure time with someone, anyone, for the first time.

She gave me an unreadable look. "You know what I mean, Nate. I'm glad you've made a friend, but I just want you to be careful." She picked up her mug, stood, and ruffled my hair before making her way to the kitchen. The sound of water running in the sink gave me a minute to figure out how to reassure her and myself.

"It'll be fine." I didn't get up; I knew she could hear me after the water shut off. It was a fairly regular thing, shouting from one end of the house to the other like heathens. It worked for us. "Aunt Susan?"

She came back but stopped in the doorway, leaning against the frame, arms folded across her chest. She wasn't going to drop it. "Nate." I met her gaze, and she looked away. *Oh.* "Nate, I'm not stupid. You've never said anything, but I know what happens at school. Kids are cruel when you're different. And, honey, you *are* different. And smart and funny and a whole list of other things that make you the greatest kid I know." She walked over and put her hand on my shoulder. "But I can't protect you from the idiots of the world, so just promise me?"

I swallowed past the lump in my throat and coughed a few times for cover. "Sure. I-I promise."

She looked out the window. "I think he's here."

I whipped around to look too. Somehow, I'd totally missed the sound of a car turning into the driveway. *What do I do? Go outside, or let him come to the door?* I had absolutely no experience with that kind of social interaction.

No use acting like an idiot; I was going out there.

"Bye!" I grabbed my wallet and phone and gave Aunt Susan a kiss on the cheek. She waved as I headed out the door and across the porch. James hadn't gotten out of the car; he rolled down the window and leaned out.

"Ready for some Kubrick?" I nodded and smiled, catching his excitement. "Get in; let's go!"

* * *

It was the best afternoon I'd had in years.

What usually happened when one took Kubrick and added him to a small town theater was that no one showed up. That weekend was no different, and it meant we had the entire theater to ourselves. We only got such fantastic movie marathons because the owner of the theater was a huge movie buff. Oh, and she was independently wealthy.

I offered to buy James's ticket because he'd driven, but he turned it down. He did suggest sharing a large popcorn for the free refills, so there was that. I wasn't sure what to do. Faking normal until it felt right seemed the way to go.

Luckily, I got my act together by the time we sat down. We scored prime seats, the ones in the middle with the railing so we could prop our feet up and slouch down comfortably. Perfect. It was likely a few more people might show up for *A Clockwork Orange* and *The Shining*, but for now, we were alone.

All alone.

Thank god, James was a talker because I would've sat there and melted into a pile of nervous goo, otherwise. We settled in as the previews were starting, and he was telling me all about the television setup at their old house.

"Yeah, my dad set it up so we could play games and stuff on it. Do you play?"

"Not really. Just never got into it, I guess." Most of the popular games were more fun if you had someone to play with, and that was never going to happen.

"You should come over sometime and give it a try."

The ease with which he put himself out there was shocking. I could never, ever, imagine myself saying something like that to another person. He reached for the popcorn, and his arm brushed against mine. It was as if sparks had lit up the theater. I tried not to react, especially since I was fairly certain I was the only one feeling it.

James fell silent for a while as the movie started. I'd seen *Dr. Strangelove* before, and it wasn't a favorite, but James had told me he hadn't seen it yet. So it was fun to watch someone else enjoy it for the first time. I tried to anyway. In the flickering light from the screen, I caught a glimpse now and then of a figure sitting on the other side of him. At some point, it shifted to the row behind us, just far enough away that I could still see it out of the corner of my eye.

I was eventually going to have to deal with the spirit, but I just wanted to enjoy the day. Slouching down farther in my seat so I couldn't see it anymore, I focused on the movie and James instead.

* * *

When *Dr. Strangelove* ended, I volunteered to do the popcorn and drinks run while we waited for the second movie to start. Of course, that was when things went downhill. I turned around from the concessions counter, and there they were: Penny Applegate and her boyfriend, Peter. He was just Peter to me. I didn't care what his last name was because he didn't even go to our school. Which explained why Penny was hitting on James the other day at lunch, nice girl that she was.

I turned away, but it was too late. The look on her face said she'd seen me. The ugly grin proved it. Great. I could let her get her jabs in now, or risk her following me into the theater. I couldn't stand the thought of James witnessing any more of my humiliation. *If I'd come here alone, I wouldn't have had this problem.* I shook my head, looking at the closed theater door. It was worth it for the chance of being someone's friend. *Now I sound like Nana. Great.*

"Crazy Nate." Penny's insipid voice drilled the words into my head. She was like a snake. Well, not really, I actually liked snakes. Fine. She was a spider. They scared the hell out of me. I set the drinks and popcorn on a table. It wasn't my first time at this game, and I really didn't want to have to wear the sodas if I didn't have to. That would be hard to explain. "Is the freak-boy all alone?"

Yes. Yes, I am. I drink two sodas at once all the time. "What do you want, Penny?" I was resigned to whatever she was going to do, but my words came out harsher than I meant them to. I just wanted her to go away. Her eyes widened, and she looked to Peter, the walking human shield, for support. Christ, he was big.

"Are you going to let him talk to me like that?" Her voice was sharp, and I struggled not to wince. Never show fear—even when I was about to get my butt kicked by a 250-pound linebacker. Peter looked me up and down, finding me completely intimidating. Yeah, right. I was tall, but I was also skinny. I was fast, but I couldn't fight my way out of a paper bag. It was why I usually headed the other way and stayed out of these situations.

I closed my eyes when I heard the door open behind me. Oh no. James had evidently come to find out what was taking me so long. I should have moved this farther away. Stupid, *stupid!* "Look, I don't want any trouble." Maybe I could still diffuse this mess. Peter stepped forward and grabbed a handful of my T-shirt, yanking me forward. Guess not.

I let myself go loose-limbed and stumbled toward him, hoping to throw the muscle-bound idiot off-balance. Yeah, that didn't work either. I found myself nose to, well, collarbone with the moron. Did I mention he was big? I didn't have to worry about it for long before my vision was suddenly filled with blond hair as James shoved Peter away. I could only guess it was sheer surprise that let him get away with it. I fell back and almost hit the ground before catching my balance.

"Leave him alone!" James didn't sound like himself. Furious, and ignoring Penny's screech of indignation, James pushed himself right up into Peter's face. It wasn't quite as difficult for him. He was a little bit taller than me, after all. And had broader shoulders. *Not that I noticed. The shoulders I mean. I should probably stop now and pay attention to the imminent fight.*

Peter put his hands up in surrender. For such a big guy, he probably hadn't met many people who pushed back. James was the exception, and it was glorious. I reined in my inappropriate glee at the situation; I needed to put a stop to things before Peter remembered he could wipe the floor with James.

Ironically, the spirit that had been following James around saved me from having to do anything. Remember when I said they glowed brighter around strong emotions? This one went supernova. It was so bright my vision whited out, and the next thing I knew, I was lying on the sticky theater lobby floor. I blinked at the ceiling for a few seconds before it disappeared and was replaced with James's very concerned face. His eyes were wide and brilliantly blue behind his glasses. I might have smiled at his blue eyes. Maybe.

"Jesus, are you okay?" James crouched next to me, leaning over me. "Nate?"

Shaking my head to clear it, I pushed myself up on my elbows and looked around. Nothing. It was gone. James was looking at me like I was going to keel over again.

"Fine." I cleared my throat. "I'm fine." I looked past his shoulder to see Penny and Peter slinking off and giggled. *Penny and Peter.* I couldn't stop giggling. It was probably only a reaction to adrenaline and passing out due to spectral overload, but James was looking more concerned to the point of panic. He was reaching into his pocket for his phone when I finally came to my senses. "I'm okay. Really. Just a little, um, loopy."

He looked at me for few seconds, considering. "Did you hit your head?" I shook the slightly throbbing cranium in question, and he stood up. "You okay to get up?" When I reached a hand up in answer, he helped me to my feet. His hand was warm and dry, and I let go as soon as I was upright. I grabbed my long-forgotten soda and sucked up a large gulp. Better.

"Sorry." Another swallow. "I don't know what happened. Low blood sugar?" James frowned at me, still looking worried. I rolled my eyes. "I'm fine. Want to go and watch the rest of the movie?"

He looked skeptical. "Are you sure?"

"Yep. Come on." I managed to grab my drink and the popcorn and make it to the theater door without swaying too much. I still felt a little odd but figured it'd pass. It wasn't like I could explain what had happened to a doctor. I led the way back to our seats and absolutely did not fall into mine. Well, maybe a little bit.

The movie had already started, but it didn't matter. James kept looking at me, and I could tell he was working himself up to ask a question. I was afraid of what it was going to be as it wasn't like I could offer any sort of answer.

"Nate, can I ask you something?" He didn't whisper because there were still no other theatergoers to disturb. I nodded and kept my eyes on the screen. *Here it comes.* "Why does Penny treat you like that? I mean, you don't have to answer but..." He looked away. The question seemed to make him uncomfortable, but I had to tell him *something*.

I took another drink of soda, stalling. "Penny thinks I'm weird." It wasn't a lie; she did think I was weird. She also thought I was crazy as hell. "We used to be friends when we were in elementary school. She didn't start being like that until we started high school."

"Seriously? She's got it out for you just for thinking that you're weird?" He shook his head. "There's got to be more to it than that."

Damn. Sigh.

"I had some issues when I was younger, and Penny witnessed an episode." Episode. It sounded so clinical, but I wasn't sure of any other way to describe it without sending James running from the theater. Sometimes, I wished I could just tell someone about everything. *Yes, I can see and talk to the dearly departed. No, I'm not as mad as a hatter. Really.*

"Oh." I could almost hear James thinking over what I'd said and deciding if he was going to pursue it any further. He shrugged. "Okay." He reached across me to grab a handful of popcorn, and his arm brushed mine. Goosebumps. *Get it together.* He munched on a mouthful for a moment before looking at me. "I don't think you're weird."

I blinked at the screen and tried to remember how to breathe.

CHAPTER FIVE

Penny Applegate drama aside, it was perfect. More people filed in for *The Shining* but there couldn't have been more than five or six including us. It wasn't enough to stop us from adding our own commentary. That movie was still scary as hell, no matter how many times I'd seen it. I caught James jumping a time or two, and we couldn't hold back the giggles. It was wonderful.

We got shushed a few times because James kept making comments to make me laugh. He was trying to make me feel better. It felt odd that someone would want to do that.

Later, we grabbed a burger at the little place just down the street. We sat and talked for over an hour. Well, James talked; I listened. He was funny, and his smile was infectious. It was like all those jerks at school didn't exist. I was...*normal*. But all good things always come to an end or something like that.

We listened to his playlist on the way home because we both liked a lot of the same bands. I had discovered Aunt Susan's old CDs a while back, and James shared my love for the Seattle sound.

The spirit had returned, sitting in the back seat, but he wasn't looking at me. Clearly, something had happened during the spectral bomb at the theater, but I hadn't quite figured it out yet. The whole thing was a guessing game at the best of times and completely incomprehensible at the worst. I would have to ask Nana about it next time I saw her.

"What are you doing the rest of the weekend?" The question caught me by surprise. I never did anything important. I ran. I read. I watched TV. Rinse, repeat.

"Um. Just hanging out at home, I guess. I have to finish up that essay for World Lit." I shrugged. "You know, the usual. What are you doing?" *Point to Nate for remembering how to converse like a normal person!*

James flicked on the blinker to turn onto my road. "I got some DVDs for my birthday but haven't watched them all yet because, well—"

I knew why. He'd told me his birthday was about a week before they moved here. And the thing that no one would talk about had also happened not long before that. When his face fell, the words tumbled out of my mouth before I could stop them.

"You want to bring them over?" What the hell was I thinking? I quietly panicked for a few seconds before he grinned at me, and it was all worth it.

"Sure. That sounds good." He slowed the car and pulled into my driveway. I saw a flash of fuzzy cat butt as Arthur beat a hasty retreat. "Text me and let me know what time."

"Okay." He stopped the car, and I had a split-second thought of leaning over and kissing him. I didn't, of course. It was a rush, though, even if I wasn't sure if he liked me like *that*. If he liked *boys* like that. I was just happy he seemed to like me at all.

It was enough.

* * *

Aunt Susan was watching TV in the living room when I walked in, and I could tell she'd been waiting for me to get home. It was kind of sweet in a way. She looked up at me and smiled. "Have fun?"

"It was good." I joined her on the couch. "Kubrick's always fun."

"So James is a fan?" Now she was just fishing for information.

"Yeah." I stared at the TV, not really paying attention to what was on the screen. "Um, he wants to come over and watch movies."

Her eyebrows retreated into her hairline. "He does, does he?" She smirked, and I rolled my eyes at her. "So, I guess you guys really did have a good time."

I sighed. "It's not like that."

"What's it not like?" Now, she was teasing, and I couldn't decide if it was annoying or not. She must have sensed how torn I was because she patted me on the knee. "I'm just teasing." See. "You don't have to tell me anything, but I'm here if you need to, you know, talk anything through, okay?"

"Okay." Yeah, I knew that.

"Good." We watched whatever zombie movie was on until Aunt Susan spoke up again. "I'm glad you've found a friend, Nate."

I couldn't keep from smiling. "Me too."

* * *

Sunday was usually a day to sleep in. No run, just a lazy morning in bed. Not now, though. That day, I bounced out of bed early and, after breakfast, looked around for something to clean. I had to have something to occupy my time. So there I was in the bathroom attacking the sink with a scrub brush when Nana decided to pay a visit.

"I'd say I must have died and gone to heaven but..." Nana grinned down at me. I rolled my eyes and tossed the brush back into the sink.

"Very funny, Nana." I pulled the plug to let the soapy water out and washed my hands. A glance in the mirror showed what my hair was doing, and I patted at it a little, but there wasn't much that I could do. I shrugged. "I clean."

"I know, darling. I was just teasing." I nodded toward the door, and she followed me into the living room. She appeared more faint there. The sunlight streaming in through the windows faded her until I could only see a glowing outline. I closed the blinds so that I could see her better. Sitting on the couch kept me from pacing, and I decided to bite the bullet. I needed to ask her about what had happened the day before.

"Um, Nana, can I ask you something?" I tried to be casual, but she looked at me with concern, so I must not have been successful.

She hesitated, studying me as if to figure out what was wrong before answering, "Of course, sweetie. Ask away."

"When I was out with James, um—" I looked at my hands. I hadn't told Aunt Susan about any of it, and of course, I felt guilty. Oh, well. "There was an incident at the theater."

"Oh, how did that go, darling? Was it a—"

"No, it wasn't a date. We had fun, and he's coming over later to watch some movies, but it wasn't...that. Definitely not a date. Anyway, there was this girl and her asshat boyfriend—"

"Language, young man!"

Great.

"Sorry, Nana." I took a deep breath and tried valiantly not to roll my eyes. "She started saying some stuff, and her boyfriend got in my face—"

"Did you get into another fight?"

"—and James kind of came to my defense, I guess, and the spirit that's been following him around got really bright, and then I passed out. It was really weird, and I'm not sure what it means. I'm pretty sure it was his brother, though. He looks a lot like him, and he said something that makes me think that was why he had to move here." I was panting a little from trying to get the words out before Nana interrupted again.

"Oh." She looked surprised and then worried. "Oh, sweetie. Are you okay? Did you hit your head or anything?" She moved as if to cup her hand around the back of my head, but all I felt was a chilly tingle. I closed my eyes and swallowed around the lump that was suddenly in my throat. I would've given anything to be able to hug her again.

You never knew how much you'd miss something until it was gone. Like the last time I was hugged. Properly hugged, I mean, with both arms. I was fairly certain Aunt Susan hugged me when I came to live with her almost two years ago, but we weren't really an overly affectionate family.

My mom used to hug me before she was scared of me.

I cleared my throat. "No, I'm fine. Not even a bump." I needed to get back to the point. "Have you ever heard of anything like that? It didn't happen until James got up in that shithead's—I mean, that jerk's face."

"Defending your honor?" Nana smiled at me, and I couldn't help returning it, just a bit.

"Nothing like that. He just knows a jerk when he sees one." She gave me a knowing look. "Seriously, Nana, it wasn't like that. Can we get back to the weird ghost brain blast?"

She rolled her eyes at me. That was never a good sign. It meant she was pausing the subject but not letting go of it. She never let go of anything once she got it in her sights. I was off the hook for the moment. Whew.

"Fine. Back to business. Fairly recent dead?"

I nodded. I honestly didn't know what I would have done without Nana. No one knew what tied spirits to us and how long they could hang around. I always wondered which time would be the last I'd talk to her. It probably explained why I never slept well. I worried a lot. "Just a few months, I think. At least that's what I've been able to figure out. Aunt Susan won't tell me anything."

Nana made as if to pat my shoulder but stopped herself. "Sweetie, it's not her story to tell." She dropped her hovering hand and sighed. "I'm afraid to touch you right now."

I blinked in confusion because I hadn't considered that. "I don't think you'd affect me like that." I shook my head. "Yeah, Aunt Susan said the same thing. I know I'm prying but—" I was going to have to either ask James outright or just drop it. "Okay, fine, but what about what happened to me?"

She looked thoughtful. "Some spirits used to make me feel dizzy, usually when the person they were attached to was agitated or angry, so that might be all it was. James was mad because that bully was picking on you and that made his brother—if that's who that was—angry. Do you know if they were close?"

"Yeah, I think so." The way he talked about playing video games, it seemed like he'd been close to his brother. It made sense.

"Well, then, there you go." Like it was that easy. *Sigh. Never a dull moment.* She gave me a calculating look. She was about to ask something I wouldn't like. "Nate, why do you think he reacted that way? James, I mean?" I was saved by the bell, er, text alert. I pounced on my phone like my life depended on it.

I know it's kind of early but can I come over now? My parents are driving me insane.

I blinked at the phone, and Nana craned her neck trying to get a look at my screen. I walked away from her and ignored the indignant look. What to say? I checked the time. Aunt Susan wouldn't be up for at least another hour. Hell with it.

Sure. Come on over.

Thanks.

The reply was immediate. He must've really wanted to get out of the house.

I looked at Nana and cleared my throat. "Um, James is coming over now. I'd better finish straightening up."

She shook her head and smiled. "I know when I'm in the way. Have fun, sweetie."

"Nana?" The lump was back. "You know I love you."

"You too, darling." She vanished.

I looked around the living room. I'd already straightened it to within an inch of its life in my cleaning frenzy, and there was nothing to do but wait. So, into the kitchen I went to put the coffee on in hopes of luring Aunt Susan out of hibernation before James showed up. I could have used the company.

* * *

The coffee didn't do its job soon enough. That was probably a good thing because it meant I didn't have an audience for the performance art I was currently engaged in called *A Study in the Casual Teenage Male.* That consisted mostly of me wearing a path in the living room carpet. Then into the kitchen. *Should I sit at the table and wait?* I sat down and then immediately got up to check the living room cushions. Still perfectly aligned. I walked back to the kitchen, over to the window, and moved the curtain back in place just in time to duck away as James pulled in the driveway. The last thing I needed was to get caught pacing, with Arthur trailing behind me.

I made myself count to ten before answering the knock on the door, and when I did it was immediately obvious he was upset. I gaped at him like an idiot, just standing there holding the door open. "Oh, sorry. Come on in."

"Thanks for this. I just couldn't deal with being at home right now." He brushed past me, and I took a deep breath before closing the door.

"Um, you want to talk about it?" He shook his head. *Okay, guess not.* "Um, let me give you the grand tour." He gave me a relieved smile, and I relaxed. That was the right thing to do. Arthur bumped against my shin, so I decided to start with him. "This is Arthur."

James knelt and offered his fingers for Arthur to sniff. He smiled as Arthur butted his head against his palm in a request for ear scratches. "Hello, Arthur."

"I think he likes you." Of course he did. It was amazing because Arthur typically didn't like anyone but Aunt Susan and me. And most of the time, I was under the impression we were only tolerated as providers of food. But he liked James. And I was putting way too much stock in what a cat thought.

"I like him, too." James looked up at me, and I could feel my ears try to burn themselves to a crisp. Living room. Movies. Snacks. Anything. *Christ.*

"Um, what did you bring?" I gestured to the bag holding the telltale shapes of DVDs. Several DVDs. Like he planned on staying for a while. I had to get a handle on myself, or I'd have a heart attack. Having a heart attack seemed more viable.

James grinned as he stood. "The theme of the day is slasher movies. Take a look." He fumbled the bag for a second before pulling out *A Nightmare on Elm Street, Friday the 13th, Halloween,* and *My Bloody*

Valentine. I raised an eyebrow at him, and he shrugged. "What? They're classics."

I laughed and pointed him to the living room. "Go cue one up, and I'll get us some soda." I breathed a sigh of relief; it was getting easier being around him. And of course, that would be the moment Aunt Susan decided to come out of her cave.

"I smell coffee." She shuffled into the kitchen in her pajamas, pulling her ratty robe tighter around her body. "Is there someone else here?"

I hissed at her to keep her voice down, and she narrowed her eyes at me. Yeah, I was asking a lot before caffeine. "James came over early." I didn't want to make a huge deal out of it, though I was making a huge deal out of it. "He didn't want to stay at home, so I told him to come on over."

She shot a glance at the living room door, and I saw a fleeting look of pity cross her face. She moved toward the coffee pot, nodding to herself. "It's fine, Nate." She patted my arm and collected her coffee. "I'll just—"

"You need any help?" James stopped in his tracks when he saw Aunt Susan. "Oh, sorry." He gave me a pointed look, and I sucked in a breath. *Oh. Right.*

"Aunt Susan, this is James Powell, James this is Susan Bradley." See, I had manners. Nana would've been proud. James put out a hand for Aunt Susan to shake, and I could tell she was impressed.

"Very nice to finally meet you, James. I've heard a lot about you." When I gave her a panicked look, she grinned and motioned toward her room with her mug. "I'll just leave you two to your brain rot. Let me know if you need anything."

That was awkward. I glanced at James and was surprised at the huge smile on his face. I blinked at him. "What?"

He shrugged. "She seems nice." He waved a hand toward the glasses I'd gotten out. "I'll get the sodas; you get the popcorn. Breakfast of champions!" I laughed out loud, surprised again, and tried not to smile like an idiot.

* * *

Aunt Susan told us she was going out; my guess was she didn't want to get in our way. She poked her head into the living room to let me know she was leaving, and I didn't remember what I said to him, but James was dying laughing. I did notice the look on her face, though—an odd mix of happy and sad—and for a few seconds, I thought she was going to cry. As I started to get up, she motioned for me to stay, finally gave me a real smile, and waved good-bye.

* * *

I told James good-bye from the back porch, waving like an idiot but trying to play it cool. Aunt Susan had returned a little while before, and as I went back to the kitchen, I knew it was coming. I was just grateful she'd waited until James left before ambushing me. Minding my own business at the kitchen table, I was working on my essay, when she pulled out a chair and sat down next to me. I ignored her as she did her best to look innocent. Finally, I couldn't stand it any longer.

"Oh my god, *what?*"

She propped her chin in her hand, grinning all the while. "I have no idea what you're talking about."

I snorted. "Fine. I'm really busy you know. Homework and things."

"And things."

I rolled my eyes and put down my pen. "Spit it out."

"I'm glad I was wrong." I knew exactly what she was talking about but waited for her to continue. "I've been worried about you—" She cut off my protest with a shake of her head. "—And I'm just glad you've met someone like James. He seems like a very nice boy."

What could I say to that? Didn't she realize we were temporary? It was only a matter of time before James figured it out and found somewhere else to sit at lunch. Then in our classes and homeroom. And one day I'd text him and he wouldn't text back. It was inevitable. But I didn't tell Aunt Susan all that.

"Yeah. I think so, too."

CHAPTER SIX

James didn't bail in the upcoming week. Or the one after. And Horror Movie Sunday seemed to be well on its way to becoming a thing. I'd gotten better at ignoring the ever-present shade of James's brother, mostly because all of my attention was on James. Yeah, it was bad. Really bad. I was setting myself up for disappointment, but my heart didn't seem to give a damn what my head said.

That was unbelievably sappy. I had a huge crush on my only friend, and I didn't know what to do about it except ignore it. Sounded like a plan.

At least at first. I calmed down a bit and kept the awkward at bay as we spent more time together. It became a regular thing to text each other stupid stuff before bedtime, when we'd talk about anything and everything. The regularity of it made the butterflies calm down when I saw him in person during the day.

Then one Saturday, he asked if he could stay over. I didn't ask why, but I got the impression something had happened at home, and he wasn't ready to tell me. And I had no idea if I should ask. Was it really my business?

James walked in without knocking—that had gone by the wayside a few weeks before—and plopped down in a kitchen chair. He looked utterly miserable.

"Hey." God, what had happened? His voice was flat and even his hair looked dejected. *Should I say something or let it go?* I just wanted to be a good friend.

"Um. Hey." *Very eloquent, Nate. You suck.*

James looked up, smiling weakly. The reflection off his glasses made it hard to see his eyes, but they seemed to look okay. Maybe they weren't as sad as they were a moment before. The smile fell away, but he didn't look quite as bad as when he'd walked through the door. "Sorry, not having a good day."

Ask. Don't ask. Ask. Don't— Oh, the hell with it. "What's going on? You want to talk about it?" God, I was terrible at these kinds of situations.

He looked up at me, and for one horrifying moment, I thought he was going to cry. His mouth did a weird crinkly thing that I never wanted to see again. James looked away and took a few deep breaths, obviously trying to get himself back under control. He took his glasses off and swiped at his eyes with his sleeve. "Sorry."

I wavered for a few seconds before pulling out the chair across from him and sitting down. Deep breath. "Look, there's obviously something going on. You don't have to tell me, but I just want you to know that you can. If you want to." *Where did that come from?*

"Nate, I—" He looked down at his hands, picking at the edge of a thumbnail.

A movement out of the corner of my eye caught my attention; his brother's ghost was standing there, looking at me. Expectantly. Like I was supposed to know what to do. I blew out a breath and waited. I wasn't going to push.

Finally, James gave me a small smile. I breathed a sigh of relief; he wasn't ready to talk about it, and I wasn't quite prepared to help him. "No, I'm—I'm good. Thanks again for letting me stay here tonight."

Relief washed over me. "So, what do you want to do?"

* * *

James loved video games. He'd brought over an ancient game console, and we played *Goldeneye* until very late. Aunt Susan took a turn or two after she came back with pizza. She was really good. I think James was a little impressed. I was too, to be honest.

Everything was fine until it was time to figure out sleeping arrangements. I was in the kitchen reloading our plates with pizza when Aunt Susan caught me to ask if I wanted her to dig out the inflatable mattress and set it up in my room. It made me stop, frozen in place and panicked.

Oh, god. I hadn't thought things through. I was a terrible sleeper. I tossed and turned all night. I was fairly certain whatever allowed me to do what I do also gave me very vivid and sometimes terrifying dreams. Night terrors were what they would be called, if I were anyone else. It was one of the reasons I'd started running. I'd wake up, covered in sweat, put on my sneakers, and go. It helped to get the bad stuff out of my head and became a habit after a while.

Maybe I'd stay up all night. That would work. The next day was Sunday, so I could go to bed early. It would be okay. Everything would be okay.

"Don't worry about it." Aunt Susan bumped me with her hip; she knew me too well and could easily guess at my dilemma. "I'm sure it'll be fine. I haven't heard you have a nightmare in a long time." I couldn't bear to tell her they were still a very regular occurrence, and I'd just gotten better at hiding them. I nodded and tried to give her a smile. *I can do this. It'll be fine. Really.*

James yawned hugely, and I had to keep myself from noticing how adorable it was. Because it was. His hair was messed up where he'd run his hands through it, sticking up everywhere. He looked a little sheepish. "Um, I didn't bring pajamas or anything because I left in a hurry." He looked at the coffee table, not meeting my eyes. "Can I borrow something to sleep in?"

I blinked. *Oh.* "Sure. That's, sure." I got up and started for my room. "I've got some jogging pants or something that will fit you." He was a little taller than me and not quite as thin, but I had a pair my mom had sent in a fit of guilt for my birthday. They were the wrong size, yet I hadn't been able to make myself take them back. I mean, she'd sent them, so she must still think about me, I guess. I grabbed them out of the bottom drawer and brought them back out to where James was standing in the middle of the living room. "Here"—I handed him the folded-up pants—"these should work." I hadn't brought a T-shirt because there was no way one of mine was going to fit him. His shoulders were broader and—*yeah, not thinking about that.*

"Thanks." He finally looked up at me. I wasn't sure, but it looked like he wanted to say something but didn't know how to start. The sadness that had followed him here had vanished while we were playing games. But now it was coming back. "Nate, I—" He shook his head. "Um, this is embarrassing."

"What is it?"

James sighed and seemed angry with himself. "I have, uh, dammit." He turned away, clutching the soft blue sleep pants. "Shit. I have nightmares. I talk in my sleep and wake myself up sometimes."

"And?" Thank god. I wasn't the only one whose brain took over at night.

"*And*, I don't want you to think there's something wrong. I'll wake up and be fine after a few minutes. I just want to give you a little warning." He still looked embarrassed and sad, and I wanted to tell him that everything would be okay and that I understood because, well, *me too*. But I couldn't. That would lead to things I couldn't talk about with anyone.

I gave him a smile. "It's good. Just trust me. It'll be fine. C'mon." I went to my bedroom where Aunt Susan, true to her word, had set up the mattress on the floor. I looked at the blankets folded at the end of my bed. "You want Star Wars or Avengers?" He laughed and some of his tension seemed to fade away.

He chose Star Wars, which made me like him more, if that was possible.

* * *

I woke up at about two in the morning covered in a cold sweat. It made me want to take a shower, but a change of shirt would have to do. I looked over to where James was still sound asleep on the floor and watched him for a moment to make sure I hadn't woken him up. His face looked different without his glasses, softer. I blinked in the faint light coming through the window and tried not to stare at the shadows his lashes left on his cheek. *Okay, not being a creep.*

Sliding out of bed and getting out of the room was easy. I stripped off my shirt and found another one in the small utility room where the washer and dryer lived off the kitchen. I pulled it over my head and turned around, thinking about getting a glass of water, when I caught a glimpse of *something* out of the corner of my eye. Then I had to bite back a yelp of surprise as the shade of James's brother winked into existence about two inches in front of my face. He scared the crap out of me.

"Jesus Christ!"

I kept my voice down by sheer force of will and the intense need to not have to explain why I was standing in the middle of kitchen screaming at nothing. "Can I help you?" He flickered back so he wasn't looking up my nose. Kind of. I couldn't help but think he must have been really annoyed that his little brother was taller than him. I didn't have that problem with Sarah; she barely came up to my chin.

His eyes narrowed as he faded in and out. "You can see me?" I rolled my eyes. I'd only been pointedly ignoring him for weeks. Of course I could see him. He frowned, and I decided to take pity on him.

"Yes, I can see and hear you. No, I have no idea why." He gave me an odd look. I was going to have to get this ball rolling before someone else woke up. "What's your name?"

"David Powell." His eyes were so similar to James's it was a little unnerving. "I'm James's brother."

"I figured." He gave me another look. "You look like him." I shrugged. "Or he looks like you. Whatever."

"Are you his friend?" Blink. It was an odd question from someone who'd been hanging around as much as he had. He saw my confusion and gave a frustrated huff. Well, he would have if ghosts could huff. It looked like he did, anyway. "I mean, are you a good friend? Can I trust you?"

What? "I haven't known James for very long, but, I guess?" I glanced in the direction of my room, keeping my voice low. "What do you need?"

He gave that frustrated non-huff huff again. "James needs to move on." David looked at me and flickered again, blinking in and out of focus. "He won't let it go, and I can't stand to see him like that."

"What do you expect me to do about it? He can't even talk about it." I thought about the aborted conversation from earlier. Did I want him to talk about it? I wondered what horrible thing had happened to David. So horrible that James couldn't let go.

That earned me a glare. David seemed to have a bit of a temper. I couldn't tell if dying made people more surly than they were when they were alive, or if it enhanced whatever anger was already there. He was definitely carrying some anger with him. "It's not what he thinks. He thinks someone did this to me, but it was just a stupid accident."

An accident. It felt wrong to talk about it behind James's back, but it wasn't like I was running the show anymore. That ship had sailed. I pulled out a chair, careful not to let it scrape across the floor, and sat. It seemed to be the right thing to do. "Okay. I'll bite. What happened?"

"Car accident. I made some, um, bad choices. It happens." Bad choices. That could mean so many things.

"What kind of bad choices?" I might as well get the whole story. I was going to feel like an ass for talking to David, so it had better be worth it. "And what does James think happened?"

David glowed a little brighter. This wasn't going to be easy. Honestly, I was tired of being the one who always had to know. Knowing how someone had died, whether by old age, sickness, or murder, quite frankly, sucked. Add in that I was probably betraying the trust of my only friend, and I felt like a real winner.

"Drugs." He was going with the blunt approach. I could appreciate that. "Nothing hard." He rolled his eyes. "Not at first. Mom and Dad found out and...it wasn't good. We had a huge fight, and I ended up packing up my shit and moving in with some friends." He looked away, staring into the darkness outside the back door. I almost expected to see his reflection in the glass, but of course, there was only me. Alone.

"How long ago was that?"

He glanced at me before looking outside again. "A few months before, um, before. I hated leaving James, but I just couldn't stand it."

"Were there other problems?" I was worried. Was there more going on at home than simple mourning? Not that mourning was ever simple.

He shook his head. "Nothing like what you're thinking. Our parents are pretty uptight when it comes to drugs. They mean well but—" He turned around to look me in the eye. "—I don't want to talk about them anymore."

All right, then. "What do you want to talk about?" It was necessary to lead some of them to talk; once they'd got out what they wanted to say, they weren't nearly as persistent.

He turned away again. Maybe he was ashamed of what had happened to him. I had no idea why. Accidents could happen to anyone. "James. I want to talk about James."

"What about him?" That topic was uncomfortable and a little intrusive. Shifting in my seat, I tried not to feel like a complete jerk.

"James won't let go." He hesitated. "I mean, I think he's a little better with the new school and meeting you"—my cheeks went hot—"but he's holding on to this weird idea that something more, I don't know, *more* happened."

"He thinks you were killed?" *What the hell?* "Why does he think that?"

"I'm not sure." David faded a bit. I waited for him to stabilize. Newer ghosts tended to react to remembered emotions, making them more unpredictable. He came back but seemed more subdued somehow. "I just know what he told his therapist."

I couldn't know this. I wanted to help, but this was going a step too far. "Tell me what you think. I don't want to hear what he said."

"I get that. It was a little weird listening in, but I really didn't have much choice." He didn't like discussing eavesdropping on James anymore than I did. Of course he didn't. He was dead after all. "He has it in his head I was killed by a drug dealer or something. What really happened was Maddie and I were high as hell and got T-boned by a truck."

"Did Maddie die, too?" That I could deal with. It wasn't anything James had talked about in confidence.

David turned and looked at me. For the first time, he didn't look angry; he looked sad. "No. She didn't."

"Was that who you were living with?" He nodded, and my stomach knotted up. Maddie must have been his girlfriend or at least a close friend.

"I loved her. Or thought I did." He gave me a small smile. "She loved me. She tried to get me to talk to my parents because she knew how much I missed James." His face fell. "I never did."

"I can't help you with that." I'd given up trying to pass on messages from the dead a few years ago. They didn't call me Crazy Nate for nothing. Yeah, I'd pretty much brought that on myself.

"I'm not asking you to." He gave me a glare. The anger was back. That was much better than the sadness radiating from him. He glowed brighter than before. Really pissed off, then. "I want you to help James move on."

"And how am I supposed to do that?" *Where is he going with this?* "What—"

"You like him." I blinked at him. How could he possibly— "I mean, you really like him." Oh god. Was I that transparent? My damn face flushed again.

"I don't— You don't—" Aunt Susan enjoyed teasing me about it, but it hadn't been put out in the open quite like that. Especially by someone who didn't even know me.

"You do. I can see it in the way you look at him." I scrubbed my hands over my face, hiding. "He wouldn't mind, you know. You liking him."

I shot to my feet, barely remembering to hold on to the chair. I was so done here. "No. You're wrong." James was my friend and I wouldn't risk that. Not on the word of a junkie ghost.

He shrugged. "Whatever. I'm just telling you what I know." I needed to get out of there before I woke up the entire house.

Instead of heading back to my room, I eased open the back door and went out on the porch in my bare feet.

The boards were cold, but I didn't care. I sat on the top step and wrapping my arms around myself; the fresh air would calm me down. I was an idiot for being out here in just a T-shirt and pajama pants, but I never claimed to make good decisions. David had to be mistaken.

I couldn't allow myself to think about what he'd said. Tonight had been the best night I could remember for years. I didn't want to ruin that. Hope was a dangerous thing, and it had no place here. Arthur made his presence known by butting his head against my arm, demanding attention. He allowed me to pick him up even though he wasn't normally a lap cat. He knew I needed it. I buried my face in his fur and didn't hope, didn't think about it.

* * *

By the time I made it back to my room, my teeth were chattering. I didn't see any sign of David, so hopefully he'd taken the hint. I'd let him talk. That should've been enough. I was crawling into bed, needing to warm up, when James rolled over. He lifted his head to blink blearily at me.

"Everything okay?" God, he was adorable when he was half-asleep. *Stop it, Nate. Jesus.*

I cleared my throat. "Yeah. Just had to go to the bathroom. Go back to sleep."

He laid his head back down, and I listened for his breathing to even out. I swear I wasn't trying to be creepy; I just wanted to make sure that he was asleep. I rolled over and wrapped myself up like a burrito to try and stop shivering. Slowly, my body heat warmed the bed, and my teeth stopped rattling in my head. I was tired and a little sad. Honestly, I just wanted to forget everything David had said. I could take care of the tired part, so I closed my eyes and finally went to sleep.

And hoped there wouldn't be any more bad dreams that night.

* * *

I could hear voices in the kitchen. It took me a few minutes to figure out whose they were. Then it all came rushing back to me, and I wanted to stay under the covers. I heard Aunt Susan's laughter and sighed. Then it hit me; what the hell was she doing up? I grabbed my phone and checked the time. Holy crap, it was after ten. I never slept so late.

I got up and hunted for some socks Nana had knit for me. They were better than anything that could be bought in a store. I only wore them around the house since they were headed for extinction; they'd have to be pried off my cold dead feet. Or something. I shuffled to the bathroom to buy myself another minute and then into the too-bright kitchen, blinking at what was waiting for me there.

James was sitting at the table, still dressed in my jogging pants, smiling at whatever Aunt Susan had just said. He looked so much better than when he'd shown up the night before that I couldn't help but grin. He turned as I walked in and gave me a wide smile. "Good morning, sleeping beauty!"

I flipped him off as I headed to the coffee. He laughed, and some of the tension eased from my shoulders. It was going to be fine.

CHAPTER SEVEN

James was a regular at the house on the weekends after that. Sometimes he would laugh and joke and seemed like he was okay. Other times, he stayed over Friday and Saturday nights, and we watched movies until he got over whatever was making him so quiet and withdrawn. Even Aunt Susan noticed.

"Is he okay?" she asked one Friday as she followed me to the kitchen, leaving James on the couch in the living room. It was another bad horror movie night, and he'd been quieter than usual, no snarky commentary. "I mean, he's—" She gestured helplessly. I totally understood what she meant, but what could I say? He thought his brother had been murdered? Oh, and by the way, his dead brother was convinced James liked me back?

Yeah.

No.

I'd been holding on to all of it for weeks. David tried to talk to me again a few times, but I'd had years of experience ignoring spirits. He could bring it; I didn't care. "He won't talk about it."

"Have you asked?" Dear, sweet Aunt Susan, what was it like in your simple life? Where people actually talked to each other? Asked questions and got answers? What was that like? I bit my tongue.

"Not for a while. I've asked before, but he didn't want to talk, and I don't want to make him feel weird or anything." I felt weird enough for both of us, whispering in the kitchen with my aunt while James's sad face was in the living room. Alone. I turned back to get the sodas that had sent me to the kitchen in the first place. But maybe she *could* help. "What do you think I should do?"

She shrugged. "No idea. He'll either open up or get pissed off." She patted me on the arm. "You'll figure it out. You're a smart boy." She grinned when I snorted.

"Thanks for nothing." I gathered up the drinks, walked back out to the living room, and set one on the table next to James as I took a seat on the couch. "What did I miss?"

"The lady just exploded in the barn."

Ugh. Wasn't upset I missed that. I watched him out of the corner of my eye; I just couldn't seem to get a read on what was going on with him. He looked over and caught me. *Crap.*

"What?" He'd turned toward me, not letting it go. I kept my eyes on the screen. Space slugs. Very interesting. Now he was focused on me and didn't look very happy. "C'mon, Nate. You keep looking at me like you're waiting for me to, I don't know, burst into flames or something. What is it?"

Shit, shit, *shit. Here goes...everything.* I looked at my hands because I couldn't look at him. "Promise you won't get mad?" Aunt Susan was right. Either I'd get him talking or he'd grab his stuff and walk out the door.

"Okay, now you're freaking me out." He turned to sit sideways on the couch, folding a leg underneath him. He reached out his other foot to jab me with cold toes. "I won't get mad. Promise. So out with it."

"It's none of my business, but you seem"—*please let this be okay*—"sad." He blinked at me, and I forged ahead before I lost my nerve. "Some days you're fine, but other days, I can just tell that—" I gestured vaguely at him. "Well, I just know. You know? And you said you were okay, but I just—"

"Yeah." He sounded so serious. I looked up to meet his eyes, and he didn't look mad; he looked cautious. I wasn't sure that was any better. "I know." He ran a hand through his hair. "I guess I'm not as good an actor as I thought, huh?" He huffed out a laugh, but it sounded flat. "Okay. I just— Okay."

He got up, and I panicked, just a little bit. *Oh god, he's changed his mind, he's going to leave. Why the hell didn't I leave it alone? Stupid ghost...* James went to my room and came back with one of his notebooks. "Here." He sat beside me, close enough that our shoulders pressed together. I took a breath and tried not to react.

I took it and looked at the first page. It was a list. *Oh no.* This was what David had been talking about. James had carefully made a list of all the things involved in David's death. And now I had to act like I was clueless. *Shit.* "What's this?"

"I've mentioned my brother—" He hesitated; his evident pain made something in my chest clench tight. "—David." I nodded. If he wanted to tell his story, I had to let him do it his own way. "He, um, he died. And

I—" A determined look came over him, as if he was forcing himself to say it. "I think he was murdered." He stumbled over the next few words. "Everyone says it was a just car accident, especially my parents, but I can't believe it. So I made that." He gestured toward the notebook.

I turned the next few pages. They were full of diagrams and what looked like copies of the accident report. Who in their right mind would have given those to him? "James, I—"

"I know what it sounds like. I *know*." He looked so earnest and desperate that I couldn't think to begin to argue with him. I wanted to hold him close and tell him it would be all right, but I didn't dare.

"It's okay." I put a hand on his arm. That one point of contact seemed to calm him. His skin was warm, and I could feel how tense he was. All I wanted to do was make it stop. "Tell me about him." I took my hand away, missing the contact immediately, but I wanted to give him some space.

James looked at his hands, and for a moment, I thought he wasn't going to answer. "He was my best friend." He moved his glasses to swipe at his eyes. "Sorry." I gave him what I hoped was an encouraging smile, wanting to help in any way I could. "We'd always been close, until he graduated high school. Then, um, he changed."

"Changed how?"

"Drugs." He swallowed hard, throat bobbing. "He got into drugs. When our parents found out, it was awful. I'd suspected but never asked. I didn't want to think about whether he would have lied to me or not." He slumped into the couch, looking defeated. "Not long before the end, you could tell by looking at him. He wasn't as tall as me, but he'd lost weight. You could see it in his face, you know?"

"Yeah." Even in my small town, we'd had our problems. Drugs weren't a huge issue, but it happened. We were talking about his brother, however, and that made it different. It was always different if it involved someone you loved.

"Then he was just gone, and I can't accept it was a stupid accident! Look!" He pulled the notebook from my hands, flipped to a page, and pointed to a line in the police report. "The guy who caused the accident sells for a dealer who'd been giving David a hard time. I overheard him talking on the phone to someone about it. He didn't know I was at home when he'd stopped by to pick up some more of his stuff." James's lips were pressed together in a tight line, and I could tell he was trying not to cry. "So it must have been planned! I mean, who does that?" He poked a finger at the police report diagram. It really did look like what David had described.

I needed to calm him down before Aunt Susan came in to see what the yelling was about. "Let me look." I took the notebook again and looked at the pages carefully. It was a simple but tragic accident. An SUV carrying the so-called rival dealer's guy had run a red light and slammed into the side of David's car. According to the report, the driver's side was completely caved in. Death must have been instantaneous. James was shaking beside me, and I had to do something. "Who was in the car with him?" The only other name on the report was Madeline Hunter. That had to be the Maddie that David had mentioned, but I was still playing dumb.

"Maddie. David's girlfriend." James dialed the intensity back a notch. "She broke her arm and had some cuts, but other than that, she was fine."

"Did she know the person who hit them?" What do I know? Maybe David was wrong, and it was on purpose.

"Who knows?" He looked at the notebook and bit his lip. "No one would ever let me talk to her. She was at the-the funeral—" His voice shook. "—but she ducked out before I could get to her. It was a hard day."

"It had to have been." I weighed my next words carefully. Things could become infinitely worse. "Do you want to try to contact her?"

The hope on James's face was heartbreaking. My guess was that so many people had brushed him off that it was odd to have someone believe him. Or at least give it a try.

"Really? You'd help me do that?"

"Sure." What could it hurt? "See if you can get some info about her, and we'll look into it." His smile made me hope we weren't making a horrible mistake.

* * *

After that, James seemed better. I wasn't sure if it was having someone on his side, or finally talking about it, but it helped, and that was all that mattered. David had been leaving me alone, until he and Nana decided to gang up on me one night.

James was staying over, and I was up in the middle of the night as usual. It was weird. James had told me he had bad dreams that woke him up screaming, but he'd never had one when he stayed over. I would know, I hardly slept those nights.

I'd just pulled off my sweaty T-shirt when David popped into existence right in front of me. What did it say about me that I didn't jump a foot and scream? Perhaps I was getting used to all the ridiculousness. "What?" I was tired and cranky and didn't want to talk to him. He made me think about things I really shouldn't be thinking about. "What do you want?"

"Is that any way to talk to a guest?" Okay, that time I jumped.

"Nana, you have got to stop doing that." I squeezed my eyes shut and sighed. I loved my Nana, really, but I didn't want to talk to her in front of David. The brush of her presence on my bare shoulder reminded me I still hadn't put a shirt on, so I grabbed one off the dryer and pulled it over my head, feeling better now that I was covering up again. I didn't know why it made me feel so exposed, besides the obvious, but I had my theories. The energy the spirits gave off was a little unsettling on the skin.

"Who's that?" I could tell from the pulse of brightness outlining him that David was anxious about Nana's appearance.

"Nana, this is David Powell, James's brother. David, this is my Nana Fran." She gave him a smile, but he just looked disgruntled. "David was just leaving."

"No. I'm not." Great. More talking. "James isn't giving it up. I told you to talk to him. I thought you cared about him."

My face flushed. God, that was annoying. "I can't just make him *give it up*. He's got to work through it on his own. He'll accept the truth eventually."

"But—"

Nana gave him a stern look that had made bigger men than him take a step back. I tried not to let my glee show, but he was about to get it with both barrels.

"Young man, I realize you're worried about poor James, but that doesn't give you the right to talk to my grandson like that." I loved that Nana was always on my side, no matter what, and resisted the urge to stick my tongue out at David. When she turned to me, I tried to look like I wasn't enjoying it all. "What's he talking about?" I rolled my eyes. "And don't roll your eyes, they'll get stuck like that."

David broke in before I could put a sentence together. "I asked him to get James to give up his crazy idea that I was murdered. It was a goddamn accident, and he just won't let it go!"

"First of all, watch your language, dear. And Nate's right, sometimes you have to let people go at their own speed. You can't force someone through the grieving process." Nana's face softened. "Why don't we have a little chat, the three of us, and figure out how to help James?"

Oh no. Panic. That was definitely panic washing over me. If David shared his stupid ideas with Nana, I'd never hear the end of it. "The three of us?" My voice did not squeak. Nope. That was not a squeak.

"Of course." She patted my cheek. It made me shiver and gooseflesh ran down that side of my body. "We just need to put our heads together."

David smirked at me. I was in trouble. "Yeah, Nate. Listen to your Nana."

"Shut it." I pulled out a chair from the kitchen table and sat. Propping my chin on my hand, I glared at him until Nana gave me a pointed look. Yep. Still worked. "James wants to talk to Maddie. I think he should."

"Who's Maddie?" She looked between us expectantly. "Boys?"

Now it was David's turn to glare. "She is—was—my girlfriend. She was in the car with me when I died." He looked at me. "It's a bad idea. I don't want her to have to go through that again."

"It's not your choice, and it's not like you can stop us."

"Nathan Shaw, don't be rude." Nana's voice was gentle as she scolded me. She turned to David. "Sweetie, I can understand why you feel that way, but I think you should consider your brother's feelings."

"That's Nate's job. Right, Nate?" He was going there. Really? That was just cruel.

"Nope. You don't get to use that. I'm done here." So done. Nana looked confused but didn't call me back as I stalked back to my room. I didn't stomp. Well, not much.

* * *

I opened the door to my room as quietly as I could and tiptoed toward my bed.

"You okay?" What was it with people scaring the crap out of me all of a sudden? I whipped around at the sound of James's voice, and he grinned up at me, his sleepy face bare. "Sorry." He yawned.

"I'm fine. Just...needed some water. Go back to sleep." I got into bed and watched him get settled on the air mattress again. That thing was so uncomfortable, but he slept on it every weekend without complaint. What did it mean?

Instead of letting myself think about it, I pulled the blanket up to my shoulders and closed my eyes.

CHAPTER EIGHT

The day started out just like any other day. I ran. School went on as school always did. The only bright spot was lunchtime with James. It made the rest of it bearable. And I couldn't lose that. David was wrong. He had to be wrong. The odds that he could be right were so low it just wasn't worth losing what we had. I'd take what I could get. If that made me a little pathetic, so be it. It wouldn't be the first time.

It was meat loaf day again. James was gesturing with his fork about something, and I was grinning at him like an idiot when it happened.

"James?" A girl's voice. James stopped mid-swipe and looked up at Margaret Kennemer, smiling at her politely. She smiled back. "Do you have the calculus notes?"

"Yeah, hang on just a sec." He dug in his bag and pulled out a notebook with a few papers hanging out. He rolled his eyes at me as he sorted through the mess. I always gave him a hard time about his "filing system," which was stuffing everything in the general vicinity of the right notebook and hoping for the best. He found what he was looking for and handed it to Margaret. "Here you go. You're Margo, right?"

"Yeah. Thanks, James." She smiled at him, and I hated it. I was a horrible person. I was just going to embrace that fact.

"Anytime." He smiled politely again and then turned back to me, fork at the ready. "So where was I?"

* * *

Things didn't get weird until Bond Day, at least for me. James asked if I'd seen the new Bond movies and was horrified when I told him I hadn't.

"That is a crime against humanity and must be rectified!" We'd been talking during our mile lap in gym. He turned around and jogged backwards, a huge smile on his face. "The new one just came out on DVD. Guess what we're doing Saturday!"

I rolled my eyes. "Watching James Bond?"

"Exactly, my friend!" His excitement was endearing. "You'll love them, I promise."

"I'm holding you to that."

* * *

He was right; I loved them. And then it happened during the fourth movie. We were sharing a bowl of popcorn when he pointed at the screen.

"Moneypenny is so hot."

Uh-oh. It was such a typical thing to talk about, but somehow we'd never had *the conversation.* The usual stuff—what I liked, what he liked, what we didn't like. Who knows why, but somehow we'd managed to avoid the subject. I just shrugged. "I guess."

I'd always promised myself I would never lie, that I wasn't going to be ashamed of who I was. I'd just never had the chance to prove it to myself. He looked at me, grabbing another handful of popcorn.

"Who do you like?" He looked genuinely curious. Here goes nothing.

"Q." I blurted it out, staring at the screen. I couldn't bear to look at him and see horror or, worse, disgust. He quietly crunched his popcorn as I tried not to hyperventilate. The crunching stopped.

"Huh," he said, "I can see that. Bond's not bad either." I turned and blinked at him. Smiling, he nudged me with his shoulder. "Calm down, you're fine." I wasn't fine. I was shocked. And relieved. He didn't care. He wasn't going to run screaming from the house. "Nate, seriously, breathe."

I sucked in a huge breath. And let it out. It was fine. We were fine. I settled back into the couch and focused on the movie as I took another handful of popcorn. Then nearly choked on it. Glasses, fluffy hair—could I have been any more transparent? James pounded me on the back and handed me my soda. I gulped it down, glancing at him. "I'm good, I'm good." I cleared my throat. "Thanks."

"Anytime." He nudged my shoulder again. "Seriously. Anytime."

I knew what he was trying to say, and I appreciated it more than I could say.

* * *

Absolutely nothing changed. It was as if something that had been living in my chest, gnawing at my heart, had been evicted. I was lighter. My runs were fun again, not just a tool to drive out all of the mess running around in my head. I caught Aunt Susan giving me an odd look one evening as we sat at the table eating dinner. I was texting with James and couldn't help but smile at my phone. She looked sad.

"Wha—?" Difficult around a mouthful of baked potato. I swallowed and tried again. "Why are you looking at me like that?"

"Talking to James?" She tried to sound casual, but I wasn't buying it. *Red Alert! Red Alert!*

"Yeah?" I slowly put another bite in my mouth and chewed carefully. "And?"

She looked at her plate, pushing the food around with her fork. *Uh-oh.* She never acted like this unless it was something that had been bothering her for a while. "I wonder if spending so much time with James is good for you."

I put my fork down. "I thought you liked him." She seemed to, anyway. Had he done something when I wasn't around?

"Oh, sweetie, I do like him. It's just—" She hesitated before looking up at me, determined. "Fine, I'm just going to say it. You like him. A lot. And if he doesn't return those feelings, then maybe you should get some distance for a bit. Because, Nate—" She leaned forward and laid her hand on my arm. "—you deserve better."

The blood drained from my face. I'd always heard that saying, but I'd never known what it meant until then. *Now what?*

Denial was *always* an option. "No idea what you're talking about."

She cocked an eyebrow at me. "Seriously? I have eyes, you know. I may be old, but I know what that look means."

"You're not old." My response was automatic. "I'm fine."

She shook her head. "Trust me, being on that side of things is not good for you long term. I've been there." I thought about her breakup with Sam and how they were still friends. Was that what she was talking about? "Just promise me you'll be careful, okay?"

"Okay." I might have promised, but I didn't really mean it. James's friendship meant more than any feelings I might have. That was enough. It would have to be enough.

* * *

Evidently, it was going to be everyone-all-up-in-my-business week. It started when James and I were walking to class after lunch. We were just about to part ways when I saw Sarah in the hall. She waved and gave me a wide grin, and I waved back. James gaped at me. I knew why. It wasn't like anyone was ever friendly with me in the hallways. I was more likely to get shoved into a locker than waved at, especially when I wasn't walking with him. He leaned toward me. "Who's that?" He raised an eyebrow when Sarah gave us another smile before turning away.

"My sister. Sarah." I'd talked about her but now realized we'd never run into her at school since becoming friends.

"Oh." He seemed thoughtful. "You don't get to see her much, do you?"

"No. Just here every once in awhile and when I ride the bus." James had been giving me a ride home pretty regularly unless he had an appointment with his mom. "I'll see her this afternoon."

"I'd like to meet her."

"Really?" I suppose I shouldn't have been so surprised, but it made me feel good inside that James wanted to know Sarah. They'd get along a little too well, probably, and I'd never hear the end of it. I could imagine them ganging up on me. "I mean, sure. That sounds, um, good."

He smiled and nodded toward his class. "See you later?"

"Sure. Later." I watched him go and couldn't help the grin on my face as I walked to my next class.

* * *

On the bus, Sarah was waiting to pounce.

"So—" She squeezed past me to sit by the window. "—what's new, big bro?"

I took my earbuds out and looked at her suspiciously. "Nothing. Why?"

Sarah stared out the window, but I could see her grin in the reflection. "Just haven't seen you in a while. That was James in the hall; he busy?" She turned to level a look at me.

"Um, yeah?" *Crap. Crap, crap, crap.* That look. It was the same look my mom got when she wanted to know who'd left the empty milk carton in the fridge. No opportunity to see it lately, but I knew that look.

"You two have been hanging out a lot lately. People are starting to wonder." She was still smiling, but there was an odd edge to it. She was worried and trying not to show it.

"What people?" Sarah was popular; people liked her and talked to her. People had been talking about me to my face and behind my back for years; I was used to it. I didn't want them to do that to James, though. He didn't deserve that.

"I heard it from Emily. Penny's been running her mouth." Emily was Penny's sister. I tried not to hold that against her because she did seem nice, and Sarah *was* friends with her. Sarah didn't tolerate anyone who acted remotely like Penny. "Is there something going on? You know I don't care who you like."

"Yeah." I couldn't look at her. I was too afraid of what she'd see on my face. "There's nothing going on, no matter what Penny says. She's just pissed 'cause James got up in her boyfriend's face a while back for being a dick."

Sarah giggled, breaking some of the tension. "I heard about that. God, I wish I could have seen it. He's such a douche." The humor drained away, leaving the worry behind. "Are you sure there's nothing going on?"

"Yeah, I'm sure." I tried not to sound bitter. I wasn't bitter, not really. It wasn't something I could ever have and nothing could change that. Maybe Aunt Susan had a point. Was it all worth it? "He wants to meet you." Changing the subject. Immediately.

"Nate"—Sarah's voice was soft—"I'd like to meet him too, but please don't let him hurt you." Damn. She was more observant than any fifteen-year-old should be. I gave her what was supposed to be a reassuring smile. "Promise me." I looked away and she poked me in the side. "Promise me, Nate." *Fine.*

I blew out a breath. "Promise." I nudged her shoulder. "Brat."

She nudged me back. "Brat." What was one more promise I couldn't keep?

* * *

I pushed the conversation with Sarah out of my mind. It'd all be fine. People would find something else to talk about. Really. I convinced myself of that until it all started to fall apart.

* * *

"So what's on for Saturday?" I poked at the sandwich on my tray, honestly not paying a whole lot of attention to James's face for once. He was unusually quiet. "You okay?"

"Yeah. Um." He looked at the table. "Actually, I have a date." His eyes flicked up to meet mine, and the bottom dropped out of my stomach. "With Margo. You know Margo Kennemer?"

It was bound to happen sooner or later, but I wasn't at all prepared for how it made me feel. I nodded. "Yeah." I poked at the sandwich again and slid the tray away, my appetite gone. "That sounds, um, fun?"

No it didn't. It sounded awful. James was going on a date with Margo Kennemer and they were going to fall in love and get married and he was going to move away and I was never going to see him again. *Stop panicking.*

"—thought we would go see a movie or something." He'd been talking while I was quietly having a nervous breakdown. "What do you think?"

What did I think? I thought Margo Kennemer should jump off the nearest available bridge, honestly. I didn't say that. Of course not. I shrugged. "I don't really, um, date. You know that."

James gave me an odd, searching look. "No. You don't." He leaned forward, his voice low. "Why is that?"

Because I'm desperately in like, if not in love, with you? Because you look at me like you see me, and not the freak everyone else thinks I am? Because...

I barked out a laugh. "Who would I date?" I couldn't look at him. He'd know. He'd know, and it would all be over. "I need to go."

"What?" James blinked in confusion. "Nate, I'm sorry. I didn't mean—"

I looked steadfastly at his ear and gave him what I hoped was a normal smile. I guess I failed miserably because he looked even more concerned. I wasn't fooling anyone, apparently. "It's fine. I just remembered something I need to get from the library. I'll be late for class if I don't go now."

He started to get up. "Wait. I'll go with you."

"No!" His eyes grew wider behind his glasses, if that was possible. I was being stupid and childish; I needed to get the hell out of the cafeteria before I embarrassed myself even more. "I mean, no. Don't worry about it. Finish your lunch. I'll see you in PE. Okay?" I silently begged him to drop it and let me flee.

He nodded slowly. "Okay. I'll see you later then."

I was heading toward the door before he finished the sentence.

* * *

The library was blessedly empty. I found a table near the back and sat with my head in my hands. James was bound to move on eventually, but it still hurt. Even so, I had to get it together and not act like a complete idiot, or he would figure me out, and then it would be over. He was fine with the gay thing; we'd never mentioned it again. But knowing how I felt about *him*? *That* would break us.

My head was spinning and I was hyperventilating. I tried to slow my breathing, but the tightness in my chest wasn't easing. There were hot tears at the corners of my eyes and, just like that, I was having a panic attack. *Breathe. C'mon Nate, breathe. You've done this before.*

"If you keep doing that you're going to pass out." I squeezed my eyes shut. *You've got to be kidding me.* All I wanted to do was panic in peace, but evidently that was not an option for a spirit-seeing freak like me. David was leaning against the table, arms folded. What the hell was he doing here? "Dude, breathe."

"Shut. Up." I kept my voice low. There was no reason to alert the librarian to what was going on. But it wasn't as if there was much chance of that, she was too busy playing World of Warcraft. "Go. Away."

"You know he's waiting outside the door." He looked down at me, thoughtful. "Oh. You found out about the date, didn't you?"

Oh my god, I so wanted to be alone. I swiped at my eyes and struggled to control my breathing. It was starting to get better, except for the vise around my heart. "I don't want to talk about it." I gritted my teeth against a hiccupping sob that wanted to break its way out of my chest. "*Please.*"

Calm. That was better. I took in a deep breath. Much better. A glance at my phone showed I only had a few minutes before the bell. Plenty of time to get myself together, but David wasn't giving up easily.

"You seem like a good guy, so I'm only going to say this one more time." David leaned down until he was nose to nose with me. "Tell. Him."

"I can't." Spirits had no concept of personal space. I sat up a little so he wasn't quite so close. "He doesn't feel that way. He's going on a date with...with *her.*" It was as if the words were being ripped out of me. David looked down at me with something resembling pity.

"Sexuality and attraction isn't as cut and dry as you'd like to think, you know." The bell rang and he started to fade. "I'm his big brother. I know him better than anyone." He cocked his head to the side. "He's leaving. Go to class; you're going to be late." He was gone.

I stared at the space where he'd been before giving myself a shake to get going. I grabbed my bag and headed to class.

I had to get it together before PE.

* * *

PE was awful. I was hoping for more running, but the gods were against me. We had to pair up and spot each other for weight training and other exercises. So, of course, James was my partner. Since Coach Morgan took up the first part of class explaining the equipment, I didn't have to acknowledge James until we had to start the exercises. He'd been fidgeting and giving me weird looks, so obviously we weren't done yet.

We started with sit-ups. Great. Not only did I have to wallow in my humiliation and angst; I had to do it while touching James. I mean, just his ankles, but still. We got into position, and I started counting them off. How on earth he was able to do sit ups while still looking at me like I was about to run away, I had no idea.

"Are you okay?" *Nope. Not okay at all, thanks for asking.*

"Yeah, why wouldn't I be?" Game face on, I swapped places with him. At least I wouldn't have to talk. His fingers were warm where he was holding my ankles. I tried to ignore the sensation, getting through the set as quickly as possible. We had to do one more round before moving on to the next thing. We switched places again.

"I didn't mean to pry, you know."

Oh. That was what he thought I was upset about. It almost made me want to break into hysterical laughter. God. It was all so awkward, and it was my fault for reacting that way.

I concentrated on what I was doing. It was hard work holding someone's ankles for sit-ups. He kept looking at me, wounded and worried, waiting for an answer. Sigh. "It's fine. Don't worry about it. You didn't do anything wrong."

"Are you sure?" *Let it go, please let it go!* I nodded, and he smiled his relief as he sat up and rested his arms on his knees. "Good. I just want to make sure we're okay."

I nodded again. "We're okay." His smile was worth the lie.

CHAPTER NINE

It wasn't okay. *I* wasn't okay. It was the beginning of the end.

I gritted my teeth at the sheer drama of my own thoughts. James didn't stay over Saturday, and he cancelled our Sunday movie day to spend time with Margaret. I didn't want to get out of bed. I wanted to stay there forever. See? Dramatic.

My phone pinged with his text alert.

Are you all right? Don't make me come over there.

God, I wanted him to come over. That wasn't the problem. I wanted everything to go back to how it was. I'd only had him for a short time, and I was already hooked on having someone there, someone to talk to. So I did the only thing I could.

I'm fine. I just got up. Have fun. I'll see you soon.

There. Misery managed. I flopped back on my pillow and stared at the ceiling. Why did I do that to myself? Why did I even talk to him? I could have saved myself a lot of trouble. I was fine. Lonely, sure, but who wasn't?

Okay, enough wallowing.

I threw the covers to the side and pulled on my running gear. I tried to be quiet because I really didn't want to talk to anyone, living or dead. On the back porch, I sucked in a breath at the bite of the wind. It was so cold my skin felt like it was on fire before it went numb. It was exactly what I needed. I grabbed my earbuds from my pocket, untangled them, and plugged them into my phone. Scrolled to the playlist named "BURN BURN BURN" and pulled my hat down over my ears. I started down the driveway, heavy metal blaring in my ears.

I began at my usual pace, warming up, but it wasn't enough. I flipped off Samuel as I ran past the cemetery and picked up speed when the

McGregor farm came into view. I kept going, pounding down the road, knowing it was probably a bad idea. I didn't care.

I ran until I couldn't breathe and had to stop on the side of the road, fighting the urge to double over, sucking the cold air into my lungs. It hurt. I wanted it to hurt. I turned off the steady blare of the music in my ears and realized where I was. Fantastic.

I was looking up the driveway to Mom's house. The house where I wasn't welcome any longer. For a split second, I could see myself marching up to the front door and ringing the bell. Wanted to see her face when she had to look me in the eye and reject me again. Wanted to yell at her that I was her *son*, and that meant she had to accept me for who I was, no matter what.

I didn't do any of those things, hadn't quite made my peace with any of it, after all. Repressed much? My breathing was approaching normal, so I turned to walk away. It would take a while, but I could walk back. I had to; my legs were like jelly. Going for a run had been a stupid thing to do, as I didn't feel any better than when I left the house.

Some days, it was better to just stay in bed.

* * *

"What are you doing?" Aunt Susan came into the room, but I was too busy being dejected to respond. Laying facedown on the couch would do that to a person. I shrugged my shoulders as best I could in response. "Where's James? I thought he was coming over."

She was annoyingly perceptive. "He's out with—" I gritted my teeth. "—Margaret." I refused to call her "Margo" or whatever the hell she thought sounded cool.

"Oh." She was silent for a moment and then came closer. Here came the pity. "Oh, sweetie." She nudged at my shoulder, and I started to sit up. She sat down where my stupid head had been and tugged me back down so I could use her as a pillow. She didn't say anything, just ran her fingers through my hair. In many ways, I wished she would just talk about it, because that gentle touch made the tears almost impossible to stop.

We sat there in silence for a few minutes as I fought back miserable tears, and she petted my hair. God, I was pathetic. I sniffled, and it was mortifying. "Please don't say 'I told you so.'"

She stilled her hand, now a gentle weight keeping me grounded. "I wouldn't dare."

"Yes, you would."

She laughed softly. "You're right. But I don't want to, so enjoy it."

She meant well, but nothing about this was enjoyable. I closed my eyes as she started stroking my hair again. It was stupid, but it really did make me feel better. A little bit, anyway.

The next day was going to *suck*.

* * *

I'm running. I feel something behind me, close on my heels, and I run faster. The sky grows darker and darker, even though it was full of morning sun just a minute ago. Whatever is chasing me is getting closer. Faster. A door appears in the middle of the road and I start to reach for it—

I woke up gasping. My shirt stuck to my skin in damp patches, and it felt disgusting. I sat up and dragged it over my head, letting the cool air dry my skin. Jesus, that was a bad one. I hadn't had an "I'm being chased" dream in a long time. I lay back down and tried not to look at the time. It was still dark outside, which was never a good sign. Something moved out of the corner of my eye, and I froze. It was nothing, could only be nothing, but my heart pounded anyway. I turned my head and let out a sigh of relief.

"Hey, Nana."

"Hey yourself, sweetie." She made as if to brush her hand over my sweaty forehead, and I shivered. I pulled the blanket up over my chest and ran a hand through my hair, pushing it back myself. Sympathy was written on her face. "Bad dream?"

"Yeah." I hoped she wouldn't ask about the dream; I wasn't sure if I *could* talk about it. I had no idea what it was supposed to mean, or if it was just my brain wreaking havoc on my sleep schedule. I drew in a deep breath. "I don't even know what time it is." I rolled over to look at my phone—*Three AM. Great.*—and saw the text James had sent earlier. The text that I had ignored:

I'll be late in the morning. Another appointment.

I hadn't answered him. Yeah, there was plenty of guilt mixed in with the little pulse of relief at not having to face him first thing in the morning after a weekend without him. I was stretched thin and exhausted.

Nana had that look on her face that meant she wasn't quite done yet. I would have been surprised if she was.

"What happened?" Blunt and to the point, that was my Nana. I covered my face with my hands. "You know I can still see you. You've done that since you were a little boy." I pulled my hands away and crossed my arms over my chest instead.

"Fine. You want to know what happened?" She nodded, looking more grave than I was comfortable with. "What happened is I'm an idiot."

"We both know that's not true." She sat on the edge of my bed, the mattress unmoving. As I said before, I had no idea how it worked. "Is this about James?"

I closed my eyes and fought the urge to cover my face again. Her observational superpowers were still sharp, apparently, even after death. "Yeah."

"What did he do?"

I blinked at her tone. She sounded so fierce it took me a moment to realize what she meant.

"Oh. No, Nana. He didn't really *do* anything." I sighed and gave in, scrubbing my hands over my face and sitting up. "He's dating some girl from school, and I'm acting like a moron about it."

"Sweetie." And here came the pity party. "It's okay to feel that way. Are you sure he—"

"I'm sure." Christ, why wouldn't they just leave it alone?

She gave me a look for interrupting. "Nate, maybe you should listen to David."

Great. "Have you two been talking behind my back?" I knew it didn't work that way.

"It doesn't work that way." See? It was still irritating. "He knows his brother. Have you ever thought about just talking to him?"

I had. I had run through every scenario I could think of, and I couldn't make myself believe any of them would ever work out in a way that ended well for me. "I can't take that chance."

"Life is all about taking chances, Nate. Sometimes you just have to put yourself out there and damn the consequences." She gave me a soft smile. "I would have never met Granddad if I hadn't stepped up."

It was a familiar story. Granddad had been friends with the guy Nana was originally engaged to. Granddad was visiting from out of town, and they had instantly made a connection. She ended up breaking up with the first guy, and she and Granddad were inseparable until he died a few years before she did. She had taken that chance, and it had been worth it.

"Yeah." I felt like a coward; I just wanted to curl up with my misery. "Nana, I don't want to be rude, but I'm going to try and go back to sleep now. I have a long day coming up."

I got that weird feeling that meant she was touching my head again. I wished I could feel her press her lips to my forehead one more time. She hadn't done that since I'd gotten taller than her, but I would've given anything to have her do it now. I turned onto my side and watched as she grew dimmer and started to fade away.

"I'll check on you later, then. Good night, sweetie."

"Night." I closed my eyes and tried not to think about what the next day would bring.

* * *

The ride to school was blessedly silent, with Aunt Susan only giving me a quick look every now and then. It was clear she wanted to say something, but either didn't know what to say or didn't want to make me more uncomfortable than I already was. The lack of sleep and general crappiness of the weekend had left me feeling terrible, as if I was on the verge of a serious head cold. Or the plague.

She waited until right before we got to school before saying anything. "Nate, you know this isn't something I would normally ever say, but if you feel like you need to stay home, it's fine." She looked straight ahead as she said it, as if eye contact would make me flee the car. "We'll turn around right now and go home."

"Nah." I gave her a grin that *felt* sad; I could only imagine how it looked. "You'd be late for work."

"No, I wouldn't." We pulled up to the front of the school, and I sat there for a moment before reaching for the door handle. She looked over at me. "Are you sure?"

I nodded, and she reached over to give me an awkward one-armed hug. What did it say about me that I let her do it in front of everyone in the damned school? Not that anyone was watching. Nobody cared about me and what I did as long as I didn't interfere with their lives. Sometimes, it was good to be invisible.

"I'm sure. I'll see you tonight."

I got out and walked into school. I just needed to get through the day, and the rest would fall into place. It would get easier.

* * *

It didn't get easier.

I didn't see James until lunchtime because of his "appointment." I had my suspicions about what his appointments were about, but I wouldn't dare say anything unless he brought it up. I was fairly certain his parents were getting serious about his therapy again. I didn't know what went on at home, but he hadn't mentioned his brother since that night we talked about contacting Maddie.

I walked into the cafeteria, and there was James sitting at our usual table. Sitting next to him was Margaret "Margo" Kennemer. He hadn't seen me yet, so I started to turn to leave—to run, *I can't do this*—but Margo saw me and pointed me out to him. So I plastered a smile on my face and went over.

"Hey—" James grinned as I tossed my bag down. "Did I miss anything this weekend?"

Margo piped up, her voice grating. "You didn't *miss* anything, I already told you, remember?" Her hand was on his arm, and I made myself sit down. She gave me an oddly defiant look and laced her fingers with his. A hard knot was forming in my chest, and I looked away.

"Nope. Just a regular weekend at home, nothing exciting."

Margo was still staring at me for some reason, but I kept my eyes on James. His eyes crinkled when he grinned. They always did that. Not that I'd noticed. I ignored Margo some more.

"I got the new Tarantino the other day. Want to watch it on Saturday?"

He didn't see Margo narrow her eyes at him, but I did. She didn't seem pleased with not being included in his plans. It looked like she was going to say something but then stopped herself. What was her deal? She'd won. She had him, and I had to live with it if I wanted to keep him as a friend.

"Sure. If you're not busy." See, I could be generous. "I missed that one in the theater." Maybe not that generous.

I stood to go and get my food, hoping Margo would be gone when I got back. Yeah, right.

* * *

Tarantino never happened. About an hour before James was supposed come over, I got a text as I was looking over our snack options. I was grabbing a pack of microwave popcorn when my phone buzzed. I wished I had ignored it.

Margo has a thing she forgot to tell me about that she wants me to go to. Sorry.

I stared at the screen. He was cancelling on me. For Margo. Again. I supposed that made sense. After all, he was the one with a life and a *girlfriend*. Who was I to be upset about that?
Okay.
Me. That's who I was. And I was pretty upset. I tossed the pack back into the pantry and closed the door just a little bit harder than necessary. A lot harder. The bang caused Aunt Susan to poke her head in the kitchen, probably to make sure I wasn't passed out on the floor or something.
"Everything okay here?" She saw my face, and I could tell when she figured it out. Her lips pressed together in a hard line, but she didn't say anything. I started to cover my face with my hands and stopped myself, settling for a vicious rake through my hair. My phone buzzed again, and I almost threw it across the room.

I'm really sorry. I'll make it up to you. Promise.

That took the wind out of my sails. I believed him. And now I felt stupid for my little temper tantrum. Aunt Susan was still looking at me like I was going to explode. "I'm fine. I'm going for a run." She blinked at me.
"You never run in the afternoon or at night. Ever." She moved forward as if to put her hand on my arm, and I stepped around her. If she tried to comfort me, I'd change my mind. Or fall apart. Neither option was acceptable.
"What else am I going to do?" I tossed over my shoulder as I headed to my room.

Chapter Ten

The sun was just starting to go down and so was the temperature. The afternoon had been fairly warm, but that was already starting to fade. I was glad for the layers I'd pulled on and the knit hat covering my earbuds. My breath steamed, and the air burned in my lungs. I ran past the McGregor farm and kept my eyes focused on the road ahead of me. I couldn't bear to see if James's car was still there.

I ran farther than I usually did, past my old house, and slowed down to a walk alongside a field that butted up to the edge of the small strip of forest between the properties. I made myself stand up straight, taking deep breaths and moving through the high grass toward the trees. It was a place I used to come to when I still lived at home. I should have said "Mom's house" because I didn't think it would ever be home again. I needed to figure things out, and the darkness between the trees in the fading light seemed to be the best place for it. Dark places for dark thoughts and all. It made it sound very poetic.

My breathing was under control by the time I reached the trees, and the muscles had stopped jumping in my thighs. I found the tree I always went to, an oak that was just the right size to lean against. I pulled out my earbuds, pushed the hat to the back of my head, and looked up at the fading sky through the leaves. It was clear what I needed to do; I just didn't want to do it. I didn't want to go back to how it was just a few short months ago. Had it been months already? Maybe two. That counted as months.

I had a choice to make. I could do what Aunt Susan suggested and protect myself, gradually pulling away from James, answering fewer texts, and avoiding him at school until he decided not to bother any longer. Or I could accept the fact that I would always like him that way, a way that would never be reciprocated, and enjoy his friendship while I could.

It was an easy choice in the end.

I had to get my shit together. I couldn't let the hurt that made my chest ache get the best of me. I slid down to the ground and sat with my knees pulled up to my chest and let it all go.

* * *

By the time I got back home, it was dark. Really dark. I'd been gone for hours, and all of the outside lights were on. Even Arthur seemed to scold me as I walked past the mailbox and up the driveway. He ran ahead and put his paws up on the door, looking at me as if to say "Well, now that you've decided to come home, don't think I'm going to miss *this*." Aunt Susan was going to be mad. She'd waited a while, but finally texted me a few times and then called several more. I'd ignored them all, not ready to talk to anyone yet.

Aunt Susan would understand, eventually, but that wasn't going to spare me the earful I was about to get. I closed the door quietly behind me in hopes of getting a few more moments of peace before the yelling started. Apparently, I had underestimated Aunt Susan's hearing because the door hadn't closed all the way before she was in the kitchen, pulling me to her in a hug.

"Oh my god, Nate. Don't you ever do that to me again." She wasn't yelling. Her voice was muffled against my shoulder as I awkwardly returned her hug. "The look on your face when you left, I just didn't know…" Her voice trailed off, and she let out a sob. *Crap*. I hugged her harder as she sniffled against my hoodie. She took a deep, shaky breath before pulling away, and looked up at me with red-rimmed eyes. And then drew back and smacked me on the arm. Hard.

"Ow!" I couldn't help it. That *hurt*. "What?"

Oh. Here comes the yelling. Arthur lurked nearby, a fuzzy witness to my execution. Because I was fairly certain Aunt Susan was going to kill me.

"What? You have the nerve to ask me 'What?'" Yep, yelling. "I texted you. I called you. All you had to do was answer 'Not dead. Be back soon.'" She pulled back her hand, and I thought she was going to smack me again, but she just raked her fingers through her hair. It looked like she'd been doing that for a while. "Nate, you can't *do* that! I had no idea where you'd gone or what you were doing. Only that you were upset"—her voice softened, just a little bit—"and I knew why, but you can't just run off like that."

I had scared her. Badly.

"I'm sorry."

"I know. I know!" She paced across the kitchen, only to come back at full force. "I thought you were going to..." She couldn't finish the sentence. I must have looked awful for her to have thought that. She took in another trembling breath, trying to calm herself. "I don't know what I thought. It's just—" She walked over to me and put a hand on each shoulder, looking up into my face. "You are never alone, do you hear me? Nod if you understand."

I nodded, not sure what else I could do.

"Good." She let me go and sat down in one of the kitchen chairs as if all of her strings had been cut. "Good. Now go to your room before I murder you right here in the kitchen. We'll talk later."

* * *

I showered first but then did as she said. I was seventeen years old and still getting sent to my room. And I deserved it. Pulling on pajamas, I got into bed, bone-deep tired. I'd just pulled the covers up to my chin when Aunt Susan knocked on the door. Well, the doorframe. I hardly ever closed my door at night; it made me feel too boxed in. I sighed and sat up, sitting cross-legged to make room for her on the bed.

There was movement in the corner of the room, a telltale flickering as Aunt Susan tried to figure out what to say. I rolled my eyes. Evidently, Nana was going to get in on this guilt thing, too. So far, I hadn't done anything to justify them ganging up on me, but I guess there was a first time for everything.

We sat there in silence until Aunt Susan finally spoke. "Nate, I—"

"I know what you're going to say. I won't do it again." Deflect, deflect, deflect. I didn't want to talk anymore; I just wanted to go to sleep.

"No. You're not getting off that easily." She sighed. "You've been lonely. I know—" She made a vague gesture as if she was as uncomfortable as I was. "I *know*, Nate. You are special and different, and it makes you a target for the assholes of the world who aren't smart enough to get to know you." She looked up at me. "You can't let it break you. It's hard and it sucks, but you're not alone. You're never alone."

"Yeah." Really. In some way, she understood, but it seemed too big, too much, to put into words. Words made it seem so stupid and small.

"You are smart and funny, and James is an idiot for not seeing that." I sucked in a breath. So we were going to talk about that. She wasn't holding back. "You need to decide if it's worth keeping him as a friend. Sometimes you need to let someone go, even if you care about them deeply, because it hurts too much to keep them close—" She shook her head. "Sometimes you have to do it to save yourself."

I blinked at her. *Let him go?* "I *can't*—" My voice broke embarrassingly, and I swallowed against sudden tears. I should have had enough of that under my tree. I thought about all the days that had blended together, broken up occasionally by a trip to town to see a movie by myself. Always alone. Always the freak no one wanted to get close to. My chest was so tight I couldn't breathe.

It hurt.

"Oh. Oh, sweetie. Come here." Her arms closed around me, and I allowed her to pull me in close. I tried to take a deep breath, but it was like I was drowning. I was old enough to know better but, damn it all, I wanted my mom. And since my mom didn't want me, this woman who had taken me in and stood up to her own family to do it would take her place. I shut my eyes tight against the tears I couldn't hold back.

Nana was there, too. She didn't say anything, but I could feel her. It was odd and comforting all at the same time. Suddenly I could breathe again. I pulled away from Aunt Susan and sat up, scrubbing at my eyes. She was about a head shorter than me, but I'd managed to almost crawl into her lap in my sorrow. It was mortifying.

It had to stop.

* * *

I took Sunday off and stayed in bed until late afternoon. I was starving by the time I dragged myself into the kitchen. Aunt Susan was watching me like I was a wild animal, as if I would skitter off again if she said "Boo." I made myself a sandwich and crept back to my room, closing the door behind me. Eventually, she'd stop looking at me like that. Sometime in the next twenty years. I still felt awful for scaring her, but I wasn't thinking at the time.

There was a tap on my door that sounded disturbingly careful.

"Come in."

Aunt Susan peeked around the doorframe. "I'm going to the store, do you need anything?"

A lobotomy? "No, thanks." I didn't bother trying to smile. It just wasn't happening. I needed to do something. "Wait. Ice cream?"

Her smile looked far more relieved than it should have. "You got it. I'll be back in a bit."

I finished picking at my sandwich and set the plate on the nightstand. Hiding in my room was getting old; I was eventually going to have to join the rest of the world.

I lay back on my bed. It could wait a little bit longer.

My phone pinged. I groped for it, expecting to see a message from Aunt Susan about flavor choices.

Still interested in watching that movie?

I almost dropped the phone on my face. Sitting up, I stared at the screen like it would magically show the correct answer. What should I do? Peel the Band-Aid off slowly or rip it off?

Rip it off.

Sure. When?

My heart was pounding. Why was I so nervous? Oh. Yeah. Total mental breakdown. That.

Ping.

About 30 minutes?

Crap. I looked down at my ratty pajamas. My hair was a mess. Shower and clean clothes.

Sounds good.

I threw myself off the bed and ran to the bathroom, almost tripping over Arthur on the way. I could swear he did that on purpose. I glanced in the mirror over the sink. Ugh. Dark rings under my eyes and everything. Maybe he wouldn't notice.

* * *

I barely made it. I heard James's car pull up the driveway just after I finished getting dressed. I'd taken time to dry my hair—so that I wouldn't look like I'd been lying in bed all day and then waited until two o'clock to shower.

He knocked on the door. I stood there staring at it. It had taken a few weeks, but Aunt Susan had finally broken him of that habit, telling him to just come in; he was always welcome. But he seemed to have forgotten all about that. I opened the door so quickly that he jumped. I didn't know what to say.

"You knocked." *Idiot.*

He blinked at me, and I said the next thing that came to mind.

"You cut your hair." *Someone please stop me.*

His hair was no longer the floppy mess he always made look so good. It was shorter and combed back neatly. It made him look older and his jawline sharper and... *Stop.*

He was still staring at me. "You look terrible. Are you sick?"

Evidently, we were both full of dumb things to say. While standing in the doorway. I moved to the side, and he automatically stepped past me into the kitchen.

"Sorry about knocking. Margo's parents insist on it. They think it's weird not to." I didn't flinch. Much. I didn't want her here. He looked at me closely, brow furrowed. "Seriously, are you feeling okay?"

"I'm fine. Just didn't, um, didn't sleep well." He gave me a skeptical look but didn't pursue it, thank god. "I was going to pop some popcorn, you want some?"

"Sure." James looked relieved, probably profoundly grateful to move past that current bit of awkwardness. "I'll get the movie going."

I heaved a sigh of relief after he disappeared into the living room. What the hell was that? I grabbed a bowl for the popcorn. Just like always. I brought out two sodas for good measure, and we took our usual places on the couch. It was going to be just fine.

* * *

And surprisingly, it *was* fine. The movie was terrible, but that just helped us along with snarky comments and groans at the bad dialogue. It felt normal. And good.

Of course, Aunt Susan finally got home, and I could tell by the look she shot me when I went to help her with the groceries that she wasn't exactly pleased with James being here. She was being overprotective, but she'd get over it.

James wandered into the kitchen to help. The chill was palpable. Aunt Susan never said anything rude, but she definitely wasn't her usual self. When I gave her a pointed look, she narrowed her eyes and shrugged.

"Cut it out," I mouthed. She shrugged, and I rolled my eyes.

We'd just gotten settled back on the couch to finish the movie when James leaned over, close to me. "Is Susan mad at me or something?"

Crap. Crap, crap, crap.

I gave him a smile even though we could still hear her banging things in the kitchen. "Not at all." I raised my voice. "She's just being cranky!" We heard a cabinet bang shut before she poked her head through the living room door.

"James, are you staying for dinner?" Her voice was overly sweet, and I glared at her behind James's back.

He nodded, but I could tell he was unsure. "If that's okay with you."

"Of course it is, sweetie." She disappeared back into the kitchen.

I could only shrug and shake my head when he gave me another wide-eyed look

"Who knows what's up?" Except, I did know. He had no idea what he'd done, and I was determined to keep it that way. "I'm going to see if she needs help. Don't bother pausing this crapfest; I'll be right back."

Aunt Susan was furiously chopping something to within an inch of its life. "I'm sorry." Her voice was low, and I hoped the TV would cover up our conversation. She took a deep breath. "I'm being silly, and he doesn't deserve that."

I leaned against the counter beside her and folded my arms. "You okay with him here?" I hoped she was because I had no idea what to do otherwise.

She stopped her mangling of the onions. "Of course, Nate. It's your choice." She pointed at me with the knife and glared. "But I'm keeping an eye out."

I smiled at her ferociousness. She really did look out for me. "Thank you." I gave her a one-armed hug. "Need any help?"

"Nope, go and entertain your guest. That movie sucks, by the way."

I laughed. "Oh, we figured that out in the first twenty minutes. Mocking it is half the fun."

"Go on then. Mock away." She bumped me with her hip. "Dinner will be ready in a little while."

I made my way back to the living room just in time to see the end credits. "Did it miraculously redeem itself in the end?"

"Nah. Trust me, you didn't miss anything." He smiled, and everything was normal again.

CHAPTER ELEVEN

I tried to keep a lid on everything when I saw them together, but it was so hard to do. I'd just walked out of French, and they were farther up the hall, next to his locker. He leaned over and kissed her forehead. Something so simple, and it made the breath freeze in my lungs. I started to turn away just as he looked up and saw me. I turned to go, but didn't make it around the corner before I felt a hand on my arm, halting my escape.

"Nate?" I heaved a sigh and turned to look at him. He was frowning. "What is it?"

"Nothing. I just remembered that—" I couldn't finish my lame excuse. "I didn't want to, um, interrupt." David flickered into view, watching the back and forth with a frown on his face. His eyes caught mine and they were full of pity. God, that was the last thing I needed. James took his hand away slowly.

"Oh."

He looked hurt. I didn't want that. I'd never want that.

"I mean, it's okay." The bell rang. "See you later?" He nodded, but I could tell it still bothered him as we went our separate ways. David gave me another look before disappearing.

So, I didn't interact with him nearly as much as I used to because Margo was usually in tow. Or towing him. Or something. Whatever it was, if looks could kill, I'd have been a dead man from the glares she shot my way. I mean, I'd never been friendly with her, but the animosity was definitely new.

And James never seemed to notice. That level of hatred, which was how I saw it, had to come out somehow, and of course, it had to happen in some spectacular way. Why was it always during lunch period? The perfect time and place where everyone could judge you and find you wanting? I'd never understood teenage drama, and I was a teenager.

I'd just sat at our usual table when James remembered he was supposed to pick up an extra credit assignment from Mr. Franklin.

James was very smart about a lot of things; however, French wasn't one of them. He gave Margo's hand a squeeze, to dislodge her death grip, and I tried not to notice. She watched him go as I concentrated very hard on the peas on my plate. I wasn't a huge fan of peas, but they were better than forced alone time with my (best?) friend's girlfriend. Who hated me. Yeah.

I'd just started to raise a forkful to my mouth when she spoke up. "I think it's time for you to move on." I put the fork back on the plate and looked up at her. Yep, definitely dead on the floor. Her eyes were bright and fierce as she glared at me, arms crossed. I drew myself up and answered in the only way I could.

"What?"

She rolled her eyes. "You know exactly what I mean. James has done his 'good deed'"—*finger quotes, good lord*—"or whatever this is, and now it's time for you to drop out of his life."

I blinked at her. What the hell was she talking about? *Good deed*? That cut me right to the core. Anger or jealousy or *something* was fueling Margo's words, but— In some way, I had always believed James would eventually figure out what a loser I was, and he'd be done. I mean, he wouldn't be cruel, but it would happen. He'd become more distant, and I'd be left on my own again.

I shook my head. She wasn't going to win that easily. "James is his own person. Maybe you should let him make his own decisions."

"And what, exactly, do you mean by that?" Her voice was icy, and I still wasn't sure where all of it was coming from. What had James been saying to her?

I shrugged. I definitely wasn't hungry anymore, so I stood from the table and picked up my tray. "Just— I don't know." And with those words of wisdom, I walked off. *Great job, Nate.*

I dumped my tray and headed for the cafeteria doors just in time to run into James. *Fantastic.*

"Where are you going?" He looked at me closely. "What's wrong?"

I couldn't tell him I'd just had a pissing contest with his girlfriend because she was insane. So I said the only thing I could think of, and I had to admit it made me feel a little petty. "Go ask Margaret."

I was okay with petty.

* * *

Coach Morgan had us doing drills the entire time in PE, so we weren't able to talk. I didn't see James again until World Lit. He was already in class when I dropped into my seat beside him. Margo was also in that class, but for some reason, she wasn't there. I looked at James carefully, and he seemed more serious than usual. *Uh-oh.* One of two things had to have happened after my flounce from the cafeteria. Either he'd broken up with her, *please, oh please,* or he'd finally realized he needed to. I wasn't going to think about that.

"You okay?"

His eyes flicked to mine, and I got a small smile.

"Isn't that usually my line?" He sat up from where he'd been slumped in his seat. "I'm fine. Just stuff."

Stuff. That told me...nothing. "You sure?"

"Yeah." He fidgeted with his pen. "Um, Nate, I—" he broke off as Mrs. Grady called for our attention, and ended with a quick "—Later."

Great. *Later.*

* * *

Later ended up being that night. James drove me home and asked if he could stay for dinner. I could tell he wanted to talk but was uncomfortable about something. It had to be whatever had happened with Margo. I probably shouldn't have said what I did, but she kind of deserved it. James didn't.

We ate dinner on the couch because Aunt Susan wasn't there to stop us. I turned on the TV, mostly for background noise. An odd sort of silence fell over us, not exactly uncomfortable, but not the easy thing we usually shared. I couldn't stand it any longer.

"So—" I pushed noodles around with my fork, still staring at the TV. "—what's going on?"

James cleared his throat and then put his plate on the coffee table. "What did Margo say to you?"

"Um." That was unexpected. "She, uh..." I didn't want to tell him. I *didn't.* It was cruel, and I didn't want him to know.

He sighed and leaned back on the couch, staring at the ceiling. "That's what I thought." What did *that* mean? He glanced in my direction and then away. "I'm not going to see her anymore."

The small spark of relief was stomped out by guilt. "James, I—" What should I say? *I'm sorry? Don't break up with her for me?* Ugh.

"It's okay." He huffed out a strained laugh. "I don't think we were working out anyway. She always said I never gave her enough attention." He ran a hand through his hair. "It was her idea for me to cut my freaking hair."

"I like your hair." I clamped my mouth shut before I said anything else idiotic. But at least it made him laugh.

"Oh, really?" He ran his fingers through it again, making it stick up in every direction. "How about now?"

I snorted out a laugh. It looked ridiculous, but his smile was back, and that was everything. "Big improvement."

He made a face and flipped me off. We both laughed so hard, and I had to put my plate down. It was the best I'd felt in a while; I hoped it would last.

Later that night, Nana paid me a visit. I'd honestly expected it considering the mess I'd been. At least she'd waited until I was in bed and comfortable before ambushing me.

"Feeling better?"

She grinned at me from her seat on the side of the bed, and for the first time in days, I grinned back.

"Yeah. I think so."

* * *

I still got death glares from Margo when I saw her in the halls, but it didn't bother me. She hadn't retaliated in any way. Yet. I counted my blessings and watched my back. She was friends, well, acquaintances with Penny, so who the hell knew what could happen. It wouldn't be the first time I'd have to be careful.

Sarah even found time to stop me in the hallway to ask about it. She cornered me at my locker, where she'd obviously been waiting for me. "What happened with Margo?"

I gave the inside of my locker my full attention. "What do you mean?"

She poked me in the side, and I twitched away. "You know what I mean. James broke up with her."

"So?" I jammed my book into the locker and shut the door with a clang. "What does that have to do with me?"

"Seriously?" She poked me again, and I finally looked at her. "You know she's probably going to find a way to blame you." She was biting her lip and looking so worried.

I blew out a breath. "Yeah." I shrugged and picked up my bag. "She doesn't like me anyway, so I'm not too worried about it."

"Just— Just watch out, okay?" I smiled to reassure her, but she still looked worried. "I have to go. Be careful."

"Okay."

She turned and walked away. It was only a matter of time. That was the bad news.

The good news was everything was back to normal with us. James still felt bad for all the times he'd had to cancel, and part of me kind of hoped he'd missed our dumb weekends together. It seemed that he had because it was his idea to have a superhero movie marathon that weekend. He was coming over Friday and staying until Sunday. I couldn't stop smiling when I thought about it.

This was so far beyond a simple crush. I'd missed my friend, and now I had him back.

Things were easier now without the anxious knot of uncertainty riding around in my stomach. Calmer now, it was no effort at all to push aside what David had tried to tell me. If only he'd gotten the same memo.

* * *

The weekend started with a stack of DVDs, junk food in the pantry, and nothing to do but drown ourselves in explosions and mayhem. After some discussion about the "proper" order to watch them, we finally got started.

Aunt Susan joined us every now and then because she loved them too. This was one of the reasons we'd always been so close. I knew next to nothing about Dad's side of the family, but I couldn't imagine anyone else sitting with us, cheering on Captain America.

Anyway, it was fantastic until later that night.

"He didn't realize that he was doing it, you know." Here we went again. David, the friendly ghost. It'd been a while since James had stayed over, and while I'd missed him, I hadn't missed these late night conversations. David was standing next to me as I looked out the back door window into the perfect darkness that only came with living in the sticks.

I played dumb. "Didn't know he was doing what?"

I turned in time to see David roll his eyes. "Hurting you. He's not all that observant."

I froze. Everything was fine now, and I sure as hell didn't need a ghost around to drive the knife in deep again. "He's not." I turned back to the window. "Hurting me, I mean."

David snorted. Well, he made a snorting noise. Thing. He scoffed. There was scoffing. "Not now, anyway. Whatever, man. I know what I saw."

"You're dead and don't see anything." Yeah, that was a little harsh, but seriously, why couldn't he just drop it?

"He'd be okay with it if you just told him."

That again. I opened my mouth to tell him to go away but stopped. How did he know? Only one way to find out.

I looked pointedly out into the darkness, avoiding David's gaze. "How do you know?" My stomach twisted into a knot. What had possessed me to ask that? "Never mind. Don't answer that."

"Are you sure?" Smugness radiated from him. "Because, you know, I could just tell you or you could continue to wallow. And pine."

"I'm not wallowing. Or pining." I pushed myself away from the doorframe and turned to look at him. "Whatever you know or *think* you know, just keep it to yourself, okay?" I didn't appreciate how he seemed to be enjoying messing with me. "I'm going back to bed."

He shrugged and started to fade. "Suit yourself. All you have to do is ask."

Nope. Wasn't going to do it. If there was anything to find out, I'd hear it from James himself. If I could ever work up the courage to talk to him. Yeah, right. Like that was ever going to happen. I slunk back to my room and slipped into bed.

"You okay?" James's sleep-roughened voice startled me. I didn't know why, as he always seemed to wake up.

I turned onto my side and pulled the blankets up over my shoulders, burrowing into their warmth. "I'm fine. Sorry." He made a noise of acknowledgement, and I waited until his breathing evened out again.

Screw David and his smug face.

* * *

Of course, I couldn't get David's words out of my head. We were back to the movies with our breakfast cereal, and I couldn't stop watching James out of the corner of my eye.

Right. Movie.

But what if David was right? What if—

No.

I can't.

There was too much at stake, and I'd just gotten him back. I didn't care how that sounded; it was true. I looked over at him. James was laughing at something on the screen, his hair still sticking up everywhere from sleep. I wouldn't give that up for anything.

Unless. What if—

I got up to take my bowl to the kitchen before I did something stupid. Rinsing it out and putting it in the dishwasher did nothing to stop my brain from continuing on its merry path to destruction. I leaned against the counter to give myself a moment to think. *Fine.*

Fact number one: I wanted to know what the hell David was hinting about.

Fact number two: I didn't want David to tell me. It just didn't seem right.

Conclusion: I was going to have to ask James myself.

Christ. How exactly did I do that? "Pardon me, but have you ever had relations with another male?" Yeah. No.

Relationships? Maybe if I got him talking about Margo? We never did talk about what had happened there. That might be a good start. Okay. I had a game plan. Now to do something about it.

"Nate?"

Shit. How long had I been standing here? "Yeah?"

"You okay in there?"

Not really. "Yep, just getting some juice. Want some?"

"Sure. Thanks." Thank god. I could do juice. "You're missing the best part."

I laughed. "Which one?"

"The Destroyer just landed." Oh. That was a good part. I got our glasses and hurried back to the living room.

* * *

It took two more movies and lunch to work up the courage to broach the subject. We were taking a break while we waited for pizza. Aunt Susan had gone to pick it up, and it would have to be now or after she went to bed. I didn't particularly want an audience for this.

Here goes everything. "Um, can I ask you a question?"

James looked up from where he'd been fulfilling Arthur's demand for ear scratches. "Yeah, what?"

I cleared my throat and hoped my voice didn't sound too weird. "What happened with you and Margo?" *There.* I did it. But now he was staring at me like I'd lost my mind.

"What? Why?"

Crap.

I looked at my hands. "You never really said, and I, um, didn't know if you wanted to talk about it or—" I was beginning to wish I'd never started down this path. Too late now. "I was just wondering."

He shifted on the couch, letting Arthur sprawl next to him, still petting his head. I was just about to backtrack, tell him *Never mind, I'll mind my own business*, when he took a deep breath. "She was too controlling." He hesitated, still looking down at Arthur. "And she was jealous."

"Jealous?" Yeah, she was jealous, but I'd never have guessed she'd actually admit it to him. "Of who?"

"It's stupid."

Arthur continued purring contentedly beside him. Dumb cat. He didn't have to deal with any of that. Feelings and ex-girlfriends and...boyfriends? *God.*

I somehow managed to keep my voice even. "How so?"

"It's kind of embarrassing now." He finally looked me in the eye, fingers still buried in Arthur's fur. "You of all people would understand." *Oh my god. Oh my god.* "I told Margo about someone I dated when we lived in Cincinnati, and she lost her mind over me hanging out over here." *Oh my—*

I cleared my throat. I had to know for sure. "Why, um, why was that?"

He smiled sheepishly. "Because his name was Matthew?" I couldn't help the nervous laugh that escaped me. His face reddened slightly. "I know. I *know*. And I'm sorry I never said anything after you—" He waved a hand at me, and I nodded, letting him off the hook. "So anyway, she was jealous of, uh, you. Because of all the time we spend together." He ran a hand through his hair. "I never should have let it go on as long as I did. She was awful to you. That was my fault, and I'm sorry."

My head was spinning. Freaking David was right all along. Damn. "No. She's never liked me anyway, so I'm guessing that didn't help." I reached over and gave Arthur a pet. "Thanks for telling me, though."

James nodded and then got a mischievous grin on his face. *Uh-oh.* "Okay, so now you know my sordid dating history. How about you?"

My face started to burn. God, this was humiliating. The truth it was then. "There's nothing to tell."

"Really?" He sounded so surprised, and I didn't understand why.

"You've seen what people think of me at school." I ducked my head in embarrassment.

"Nate, I—" I could hear the sadness in his voice and so didn't want to be the cause of it. I wasn't a broken thing even though sometimes I felt like it.

"Don't. I don't let them bother me, and you shouldn't either." And then, thank god, I heard Aunt Susan pull up in the driveway. "Enough deep conversation for now, okay?"

"Yes, please." James laughed and everything was fine again. "We should tell her she missed Loki again."

"I value my life too much. You're on your own." I easily caught the cushion he threw in my direction. "Pizza?"

He jumped up and headed to the kitchen in answer.

* * *

Later, after Aunt Susan had gone to bed, James brought up dating again. "Can I ask you one more question? About what we were talking about earlier?"

What? "Earlier?" *Oh.* "Um, sure..."

"I was wondering—" He stopped, and I turned toward him completely, pausing the movie. What else could he possibly want to know? "Um. You said you've never dated anyone. Does that mean you've never kissed anyone?"

I was doing either a very good or very bad impression of a goldfish at the moment. "What? I— Uh." I cleared my throat and tried very hard not to topple off the couch. "No. No, I haven't." Why? Why would he ask that? Did he want to— *No. Stop.*

He reached over and picked up the remote. "I was just wondering." He gave me a bright smile as if he hadn't just tilted the world on its axis. "No big deal. Thanks for telling me."

"Okay?" I blinked at the screen and said the only thing that made sense at the moment. "You going to hit play or what?"

CHAPTER TWELVE

We didn't talk about it again. It was as if the conversation had never happened. And I wasn't sure what to think. I was trying very hard not to obsess about it, but I was *really* obsessing about it. Why would he ask that? Any of it?

And what the hell was I supposed to do with the other *thing*? Besides avoid David's smug, glowy face at all costs; that was a given.

I was so busy *not* obsessing about it that I didn't notice when James walked up to our table. I jumped about a foot when he threw his books down.

"Jesus! Jumpy much?" His tray clattered on the table as he sat down, and his grin took the sting out of his words. Because I *was* jumpy. I was on edge because now there might be a chance, and he had no idea how I felt about him.

"Sorry." I picked up my fork, but I didn't really want to eat. My stomach had a brand new knot in it that wouldn't go away.

He poked at his lunch for a moment and then looked up at me. "Do you want to take a ride into Cincinnati with me sometime during Christmas break?"

"Sure." I hadn't been to the city in a long time. It'd be fun to go there with James. "Why?"

He fiddled with his fork again before putting it down. "I found Maddie." It took me a moment before placing the name. Not a fun time after all. He leaned forward, speaking quickly, supposedly before I could say anything to try to talk him out of it. "I just want to know. I mean, I need to know for sure what happened, and she's the only one— She was the last one who—" The earnestness on his face was heartbreaking.

"Yeah, okay." I knew more than I should, unfortunately, which was why I had to go with him. "When do you want to go?"

"The day after Christmas. Mom and Dad are going to visit some friends, so they won't be around." His relief at my easy acceptance was clear. "Can you go?"

"I don't see why not. I'll make sure, though, okay?" I was going no matter what. He smiled gratefully at me, and I felt like the biggest jerk in the world.

* * *

Christmas break arrived with little fanfare. I was looking forward to the two weeks out of school, despite what was coming. I just couldn't let on that I knew.

Aunt Susan told me to invite James over on Christmas for Chinese food and to watch *A Christmas Story*. What could I say to that? It was tradition. Also traditional were the presents Aunt Susan and I got each other. I got an allowance for saving her from having to get a cleaning service, next to impossible out here, so I always got her a gift card to load up her e-reader, and a movie or two I thought she'd like. She'd get me a gift card to buy more music online and actual paper books. It worked.

I also got Sarah a boxed set of some British detective show she was crazy over. We wouldn't get to exchange gifts until we went back to school. She always got me something funny, so I couldn't wait to see what she came up with.

And now there was another person to buy for. Thank god for Amazon. I got James a T-shirt from one of the movies we had watched on our marathon weekend, nothing too expensive. I totally didn't agonize over it for hours until Aunt Susan finally ran out of patience. "For god's sake, Nate, it's a freaking T-shirt, not a ring. Just buy it already."

So. Not a big deal at all.

He loved it, so I guess it was a good choice. He gave me some CDs I'd been keeping an eye out for but hadn't been able to find. They were secondhand, so it meant he went and actually looked for them. I managed not to make too big of a fool of myself over them, but they were pretty cool.

When I told Aunt Susan we were going to go to Cincinnati the day after Christmas to hang out, she looked at me funny. It was like she knew I wasn't telling the entire truth but wouldn't call me out on it. I didn't like lying by omission, but I didn't want to break James's trust any more than I already had.

* * *

The drive into the city was fairly uneventful. Traffic was bad, but that was to be expected the day after Christmas. James was very quiet, which also was to be expected. I glanced in the mirror and saw David in the backseat, looking resigned instead of the anger that I was expecting.

"So, what's the plan?"

James sighed. "She's living with her sister not far from where they...where *she* used to live. So, I figure we'll just go and ring the doorbell."

"Seriously?" I glanced back at David again, and he rolled his eyes. It was a terrible plan. "What are we going to do when she calls the cops?"

"She's not going to call the cops."

"You can't know that!" I turned to look at him, trying hard not to stare at David's flailing form in the backseat.

James's shoulders slumped, and he looked so defeated I had to say something else. "Okay, maybe she won't."

David was practically having fits now. It was hard to ignore him, but I continued on.

"I mean, I hope she doesn't, but I just want to make sure you're prepared for her to have a bad reaction to you just showing up."

"Don't you think I know that?" He immediately looked contrite. "Sorry. I just— I have to know. I need to talk to someone who was there." He sighed again. "If you've changed your mind, I can find a coffee shop or somewhere you can hang out."

I looked out the window, avoiding both David and James. "I'm not letting you go alone."

"Thanks, Nate."

It was such a bad idea.

* * *

Maddie didn't call the cops, but it was a close thing. She answered the door when James knocked and started shaking her head as soon as she saw him. "No. I told you no."

Had he contacted her before? He was doing everything but sticking his foot in the door to get her to wait. "I'm sorry. You said you didn't want to talk about it, but"—he sounded desperate, and I could see her face soften—"Maddie, please."

It was odd standing out in the hallway, watching it all play out. So many different emotions were warring on Maddie's face that I was certain she was about to tell us to get the hell out. She didn't. She looked infinitely unhappy, her lips pressed together in a line, but she stepped back to let us in. I didn't miss the curious look she gave me as I awkwardly followed on James's heels.

Common courtesy took over, and she gestured for us to take a seat on a worn but clean couch. She sank down into a chair, tucking long dark hair behind her ear. She was pretty with delicate features, but I could see a hardness in her that was made from grief and mourning.

David blinked into existence behind her left shoulder, the pain and sadness radiating off him palpable. I tried not to stare directly at him, aware that his emotions were going to be just as much on display.

Maddie looked away, and her face was set in lines of determination before she met James's gaze again. "Okay, fine. You're here. Ask your questions."

James drew in a sharp breath. He looked uncertain, as if now that he actually had her attention, he had no idea where to begin. We were sitting side by side on the couch, so I pressed slightly closer to him, making our shoulders touch. He looked down at his hands, and I started to pull away, but then he leaned into me as well. Okay. This I could do.

"Can you tell me what happened that night?"

Maddie made a frustrated noise. "You know what happened. You read the police report."

I could feel James stiffen. "I want to hear it from you." His voice was very, very careful and restrained. I leaned into him again, and he relaxed just a bit.

She huffed out a breath before answering. "We got hit by a car, and David died." The blunt words were cruel but resigned. How many times had she told her story? "What else do you want me to say?" She slumped in her chair, her brave face fading.

"No. There has to be more to it than that." James scooted forward, pulling away so he could get closer to Maddie. "I mean, the guy who hit you worked for a drug dealer, right? I overheard David talking—"

"No, he didn't! That's what this is all about?" Her eyes shone with something akin to pity. "James. It was an accident. The guy's name was similar to someone David used to buy from, but that's all. I swear to god that's all." Her eyes filled with tears and David made an abortive move towards her shoulder. "God, don't you think I would have done anything if I'd thought there was something else behind it?" She scrubbed her hands over her face, taking a deep breath. "Whatever you have in your head about what you think happened, it's *wrong*. Just let it go."

"No." He slid back, shaking his head, and I could feel a tremor run through him from where he was again tightly pressed against me. "I can't— Maddie, I—" She reached over and squeezed his arm. He leaned back, pulling away from both of us, and slumped into the couch. "Are you sure?"

"I'm sure."

James stood, and I scrambled up with him. In about five minutes, Maddie had completely decimated everything he'd been holding onto for months. And now I had to help him hold it together until we got home.

He faced Maddie, his body stiff. "I'm sorry to have bothered you." She nodded, and he walked to the door. David was still standing behind where Maddie was seated in the chair. He was watching me pointedly and finally spoke when I started to follow after James.

"Say something for god's sake!" David was in my face. I turned my head, not looking at him because I was so beyond caring. James was at the door, obviously waiting for me. My gaze on the floor, David had to duck his head to make me look at him. "*Please.*" I closed my eyes for a second before turning to Maddie.

"I'm very sorry for your loss. Um. Thanks for talking with him."

She didn't smile, but her eyes were kinder than they had been. She lowered her voice. "What's your name?"

"Nate."

She nodded. "Okay. Nate. Take care of him, will you?"

I glanced at James's back. "I will." I walked to where James was waiting and reached past him to open the door, holding it for him. "Let's go, all right?"

He didn't speak as we descended from Maddie's apartment on the second floor, our footsteps echoing in the stairwell. I followed him out the door of the building to the sidewalk below. He managed another block before he turned into a small alleyway next to a coffee shop, obviously familiar with the area.

I followed him without question, waiting for the eventual breakdown. He wasn't crying or doing anything that would be obvious, but he leaned heavily against the rough brick wall before sliding down it into a crouch. He buried his face in his hands, and I waited. He didn't sob or wail and was totally silent until he suddenly slammed his palm flat against the pavement. I jumped at the movement, and he did it again. And again. And again, but with a closed fist.

Enough. I stepped forward without thinking and went to my knees in front of him, not caring about the dirt on the asphalt. "*Stop.*" I grabbed his arm and ran my hand down it to cradle his hand gently, looking to see if he'd broken skin, touching the edge of the scrape found there.

He stared at my hand on his as if he'd never seen it before. Self-conscious, I started to pull away, but he closed his fingers around mine, stopping me. My breath caught; I didn't move. When he bowed his head, I leaned toward him, comfort the only thing on my mind. I'd never been so close to him before. We'd sat on a couch, side by side, but I'd always been careful not to get too close, not to cross that line.

His hair was soft against my cheek. I closed my eyes, letting him lean against me. He still had my hand in a tight grip, and I wove our fingers together, careful of the scrape on side of his palm. Of all the times I'd allowed myself to think of holding him close, I'd never imagined anything like this. A fine tremor ran through him, and I didn't hesitate, wrapping my arm around his shoulders and pulling him close.

He was warm even though it was cold out. The frigid damp seeped through my jeans where my knees touched the rough pavement, but I didn't care. We didn't speak as I held him together while he shook apart.

* * *

I lost track of how long we stayed like that, but eventually we had to move. His fingers loosened, and I took that as my cue to back away, allowing my lips to brush his hair as we pulled apart, a ghost of a kiss without acknowledgement.

He cleared his throat and got to his feet. "Thanks."

"Anytime." When he offered a hand up, I took it and then tried to brush the majority of the dirt off my knees. It really didn't help. I ran a hand through my hair and looked toward the busy street that had existed beside us the entire time. "Um, you hungry?"

James's grateful look told me I'd done exactly the right thing. He shrugged. "I could eat." He bumped my shoulder and led the way toward the sidewalk. "There's a burger place about two blocks away that's really good."

"Let's go."

* * *

The burgers really *were* good. James grinned at me with his mouth full, and I tried not to choke on my chocolate shake, laughing. He had mustard on his face and looked...happy.

"Oh my god. You've got something right—" I gestured to my own face, and he missed it with his napkin completely. I rolled my eyes and reached over to clean him off. He grinned at me; my chest felt like it could burst. I didn't want to break the spell, but David was whispering in my ear.

"He's good at hiding. Don't let him. You have to make him talk it out."

I flicked my hand next to my ear, as if shooing away an annoying fly, and nodded. I knew it, and he knew that I knew it, but I didn't want to do it, not yet. We were going to have to go home soon, and I wanted to hold on to that moment for just a little bit longer. James gave me a searching look that made me wonder what he saw.

"I'm okay, you know. Just in case you were wondering." He popped the last bite of burger in his mouth and chewed at me defiantly before swallowing. "I'm fine."

"I know." I met his eyes, willing him to believe me. "And if you're not, you will be."

He looked surprised and then smiled. "Thanks."

And with that, David finally looked satisfied and faded away. For the moment.

* * *

"I'm not telling anyone what happened today. Especially not my parents." He glanced at me, taking his eyes off the road for a second, waiting for my response.

"That's probably best." We were still about half an hour from home, so I jumped in feet first. "What are you going to tell your therapist?" His hands tightened on the wheel, and I wondered if I'd gone too far. He'd mentioned his therapist a few times, but David had told me more about it than James had.

"I'll handle it. Convince them I'm not crazy after all."

His smile was strained, which only made me want to assure him he'd never been crazy; he was only hurting and looking for someone to blame. How did you tell someone that?

I looked out the window and considered my words carefully. "You weren't." He looked at me questioningly. "Crazy, I mean. You wanted answers. There's nothing wrong with that." I fiddled with the radio. "It must suck to be so normal."

He laughed, and I chuckled along with him. "Thanks, Nate." He reached over and squeezed my shoulder. "Seriously."

Chapter Thirteen

We still had a few days left of Christmas break, so we spent them at my house lazily watching movies or reading, just spending time together. I caught James looking at me a few times, but I didn't allow myself to imagine what that might mean. From the way he looked away each time I met his eyes, I had no idea if *he* even knew. Things had been a little weird since we'd gotten back from our trip to the city. Not bad weird, really, just different. James seemed more—for lack of a better word—settled, for some reason. The whole David thing had weighed him down so much, and now I was finally seeing the "real" James—seeing the guy who wasn't constantly wondering who'd stolen his brother away from him.

It was nice.

He laughed more easily and was a little bit freer with his smiles. It made something twist in my stomach I thought I'd managed to beat into submission. Those butterflies were more resilient than I thought.

I had a passing thought to ask why he never wanted to hang out at his house but couldn't bring myself to do it. David had only told me that their parents were "uptight." I had no idea what that was about. Was it only about the drugs? I had no clue if they knew James was bisexual or if they cared. He seemed pretty comfortable with it, not that we'd ever talked about it again.

And there was James's uncle, Sam. Everything Aunt Susan had said about him made him appear to be pretty open-minded. He would have to be since she had dated him. So that couldn't be the issue.

I wanted to talk about it. I wanted to know anything and everything about him. I wanted to know why he looked at me like that and what he was thinking when he did.

I didn't say anything.

* * *

James had gone home for the day—he had to go home sometime—and of course Aunt Susan ambushed me over dinner to suggest I invite him to ring in the New Year with us. It wasn't my choice, but there'd be no stopping her once she'd gotten an idea in her head.

"We haven't done anything for New Year's since you moved here," she had said, pointing at me with her fork. "James would probably come over, too. It's like he practically lives here now."

My ears turned pink; I could feel them burning. "Maybe—"

"I don't remember asking your opinion." She speared another bit of potato and popped it in her mouth. "If you don't watch it, I'll break out the shiny party hats."

"You wouldn't dare!" My gasp was half-joking and half-worried. She totally would have done something over the top to embarrass me if I didn't play along. I sighed heavily, acting completely put out. "Fine. Have it your way."

She'd grinned in triumph. "See. That wasn't so hard."

Of course, he wanted to do it. He'd sounded excited about it, and I'd been worrying ever since. I didn't know why I was so worried; we seemed to be moving toward something more solid. But things were still fragile enough to fly apart if I wasn't careful. Plus, everyone always made stupid resolutions for the New Year. I wanted to do something different.

I wanted to tell him; I wanted to tell him everything. But the prospect of doing that was so terrifying I couldn't bring myself to think about it too closely. I wished I had someone to talk to about it, but of course, my current social circle consisted of James (duh, no), my aunt (maybe, probably), my dead grandmother (another possibility) and James's dead brother (a resounding NO).

So what to do? I had no idea.

Here's to the New Year, I guess.

* * *

A couple days before New Year's, James asked me some questions I couldn't answer. I was lying on the couch reading a book I'd been meaning to get to for years, not paying attention to anything else going on. James said something, poking me in the leg to get my attention.

"Hello? You in there?" He waved a hand in front of the page. "Did you hear a word I said?"

I batted his hand away and closed the book, holding a finger in it to keep my place. "I am terribly busy reading a tale of high adventure. What?"

He rolled his eyes, quirking a smile at me just the same. "I asked if you had a chance to see your sister yet. Does she get to come over here? I mean, you said that you see her at school but—" His face was bright and open because he didn't really know what he'd just asked.

See what a mess the whole situation was? James was asking me something that should be simple, but it wasn't, and now I had to lie.

"Um—" I carefully put my book on the table, reaching past where James was sitting on the floor against the couch. I knew this would eventually come up. "—no. She's not allowed."

"Oh." His face fell. "I'm sorry, that must be pretty tough." I was concentrating on the ceiling now but still felt his gaze on me, watching for a reaction. "She waved at me in the hallway the other day."

"Really?" That certainly sounded like Sarah. It was probably her way of telling him she knew exactly who he was and that she was keeping an eye out.

"She seems pretty popular." He shrugged. "People talk, you know?"

I wondered exactly what people had been saying to him. It rubbed me the wrong way immediately.

"Yeah, they certainly do." It came out more harshly than I meant for it to. Those people had made my life a living hell for years. What right did they have to try to poison someone outside of their precious little circle? To breed more hatred just because someone didn't fit into their tiny little box? James was staring at me. I closed my eyes so I wouldn't have to see the pity wash over his face. "Sorry."

"No, it's okay." He was silent for a moment. "If I ask you something, will you promise not to get mad?" I stared at him. There was no pity to be found, only simple concern and curiosity.

"I can try." My heart started to pound. "I make no promises, though."

He nodded. "Did your mom kick you out because you're gay?" I blinked back up at the ceiling; I couldn't look at James, though his voice was gentle. "I just wondered why you live with Susan." He held his hands up. "Not that I don't like her, she's very cool, but you have to admit it's a little odd when your mom lives in the same town."

Great. For a split second, I wished I had some horrible reason that was at least believable. Because I was one of the lucky ones; my mom knew before I did. I came out to her when I was fourteen, and while she was wary of my "ability," she was accepting of that other part of who I was. So my being gay was never a problem.

James was still looking at me—probably afraid he'd gone too far or had offended me. As if he could do either. But I couldn't tell him the truth.

I shook my head. "Nothing like that. She's cool with it." I sighed at the ceiling. This was the hard part. "I can't, um, I can't really say why. She has her, um, reasons." I turned to look at James, and he just nodded.

"I understand. You don't have to tell me if you don't want to."

God, I wanted to. I wanted someone outside my immediate family I could share the craziness with. I wanted that so badly it made my chest ache.

"I'm sorry."

He leaned his head back against me from his seat on the floor, and I was sure he could hear my heart trying to escape. This was also something new. He had become more physically affectionate since that day in Cincinnati. Nothing over the top—a hand on my shoulder, ruffling my hair, that kind of thing.

He smiled at me. "Nate, seriously, it's fine. I get it." He turned his head so he could look at me sideways. "Just take your own advice, okay? If you ever want to talk about anything, I'm here."

I swallowed past the lump in my throat. We'd just had a moment, and it wouldn't be good manners to burst into tears.

"Things were—" I stopped to clear my throat. "Things were very hard for a long time." I stared at the ceiling, blinking furiously. "But they're better now, you know?"

I could still feel his gaze on me and the warmth of his head against my arm.

"You mean with people at school?"

"Yeah." I wanted to tell him it was all because of him. I *thought* he knew; I *hoped* he knew.

"I'm glad."

I moved finally and squeezed his shoulder. He *had* to know. "Want to watch a movie or something?"

The moment passed, but we stayed next to each other like that for the rest of the afternoon.

* * *

"You want to what?" Aunt Susan was looking at me like I'd lost my mind. "Are you insane?" I was afraid she would say that. It was the most terrible idea of all terrible ideas. She sat at the kitchen table, coffee mug in hand. "Okay, okay, okay. Give me a second." She ran a hand through her hair and blew out a breath. "Run me through it again. What *exactly* do you want to tell him?"

"I want to tell him everything."

"Everything?" She sighed when I nodded. "Nate, I just don't know. I mean, are you sure?"

"Not in the least little bit." I pulled out the chair next to her with a scrape, sat down, and put my head in my hands. "I'm terrified of what he might say, what he might think." I peeked at her through my fingers. "What the hell am I going to do?"

She took another drink of coffee. "You're going to hate me for saying this, but—" She looked into her mug. "I can't tell you what to do." I groaned and lay my head on the table, giving it a thump for good measure. She smacked me on the back of the head. "Stop that. Fine. Here's what I *think* you should do." I rolled my head to the side so I could see her. "First of all, you need to talk to your Nana." I sat up, and she continued before I could say a word. "Talk to her and ask her about it. She's the only one who's experienced it firsthand. Then—" She got up to pour another cup of coffee. "—you need to go with your gut."

I dropped my head to the table again. "Go with my gut? That's your advice?"

"Hey!" Her voice was sharp, but I didn't pick my head up that time. "I said talk to Nana first, you brat. Go do that, and we'll talk about it some more." She walked to the table, and instead of the smack I was expecting, she put a warm palm on the back of my head. "Okay?"

I heaved out a breath. "Fine. I'll talk to Nana." She patted me on the head like a puppy. "Stop that, I feel like a dog."

"Tough." She yawned and headed back to her room. "No more serious conversations before ten AM. New rule."

I smiled to myself despite the whirling thoughts in my head. Also, I felt a bit sick. Maybe I should go back to bed too.

* * *

I ended up crashing on the couch and flipping through channels, as one did when one was experiencing severe emotional turmoil. Maybe it was my emotional turmoil that helped to summon Nana, because otherwise, I have no freaking clue what pulled her from nowhere.

"Bad day?"

I almost fell off the couch.

I clutched the throw pillow under my head to keep it from sliding off as well and looked up into Nana's concerned face. "Is there any other kind?"

"Don't be like that," she tutted. "You've had some good ones lately, right? I mean, James has barely left the house. I'm surprised he's not here right now."

"He had to go home for a while. His mom said." I blurted this out without thinking and pulled the pillow up to try to smother myself. Or at least stop myself from talking further. "He'll be back tonight for New Year's." My voice was muffled, so the pillow was failing miserably. I flung it to the other end of the couch.

Nana was grinning at me, and I rolled my eyes and shrugged. She laughed. "I see."

"Speaking of James"—I needed to get this over with, and it was the only way to stop her from making fun of me—"I need to talk to you about something. Something, um, important." That got her attention.

"Is it serious?"

I shuffled my legs to the side as she sat. She would have gone right through them, but it felt really weird.

"Kind of." Here went nothing. "How did you tell Granddad about your ability?"

"Ah. I was wondering when this would come up." Nana was always one step ahead of me, so I wasn't surprised she saw that on the horizon. "It certainly helped that it was pretty much love at first sight." She waggled her eyebrows.

"Anyway, it wasn't easy, that's for sure. Granddad didn't believe me at first, thought I'd lost my mind." She looked at her hands, remembering. "It took some convincing but he finally came around. We didn't talk about it much after that. He would turn a blind eye when *things* happened." She looked up at me again. "Does that help?"

I covered my face with the pillow again and groaned. "Not really." Clutching it to my chest, I looked over it at her. "I mean, I'm glad it all worked out eventually for you, but I just don't..." I hated being so indecisive.

"You have to go with your gut, sweetie."

"That's what Aunt Susan said." I squeezed the pillow tighter. "My gut wants to puke."

She laughed. "I can understand that. But—" She was serious again. "If you want James in your life, and you feel this is something you need to tell him, and you're absolutely sure you need to tell him, then"—she spread her hands—"you've already got your answer."

I rolled toward the back of the couch and buried my face in the cushion.

* * *

That night, thankfully, Aunt Susan didn't follow through with her threat of shiny party hats after all. It was, well, nice. I mean, we didn't have caviar and champagne, but our pizza bites and chips and dip were really good. James came over around ten after spending time with his parents, at their request, and for the first time in forever, he seemed happy after being at home. It was a relief.

It didn't help my anxiety, though. I was going to do it. I was going to tell him. Call it a New Year's resolution. Which meant I was giving myself until the end of Christmas break to spill my guts. I wasn't going to tell him tonight, hell no, but just making the decision felt like I was going to burst into flames at any moment. Besides, there was no way I was going to tell him while Aunt Susan was around.

We put on the silly countdown show, and all three of us sat on the couch to make fun of it. It wasn't a tight fit, but somehow James and I ended up sitting close to each other with shoulders pressed together. He didn't move away, and I didn't want to try to figure out what that meant. I couldn't, not with this huge, self-imposed deadline hanging over my head. The warm feeling in my stomach from having him so close was far more enjoyable.

When midnight was almost at hand, Aunt Susan ducked into the kitchen and came back out carrying three juice glasses with about an inch of champagne in each. It was nothing if not classy. She handed each of us a glass and shrugged. "Don't get any bright ideas; this is special occasion only champagne." James grinned at me, and I smiled just as goofily back at him.

"Three..." As the countdown started, we all stood in the middle of living room, watching the ball drop on Times Square.

"Two…" I pulled my eyes away from the screen; all I could focus on was the way the soft glow of the Christmas lights lit up his face. He glanced at me and smiled as we counted down.

"One! Happy New Year!" We clinked our juice glasses together and took a sip. James and I both grimaced at the taste, but we drank it anyway. It was kind of awful.

James held his glass up again, looking into my eyes. "To new friends."

I tapped my glass against his and Aunt Susan did the same. I couldn't miss her smile as we drank the last little bit, making faces the whole time.

"Come here, you." Aunt Susan gave me a hug and then did the same to James, giving us each a kiss on the cheek. "It's been exciting and all, but now I'm going to bed. We'll clean up in the morning." She waved at us absently as she wandered off to her room.

I set my empty glass on the table. James did the same with a little *thunk* and turned to me. "Nate?" I looked at him, but I couldn't read the expression on his face.

"Yeah?"

He didn't say anything, just moved closer, and before I could respond, he was hugging me. My arms automatically came up to hug him back. We stood there for a few moments, me in utter shock. Then he finally pulled back but kept his hands on my shoulders. "You okay?"

I had a quick second of panic, thinking he was going to do something crazy like kiss me, but it was only wishful thinking. He squeezed my shoulders.

"Happy New Year, Nate." And then he let me go and grabbed up our glasses to take them to the kitchen.

I watched him go, alone now in the living room. "Happy New Year, James."

* * *

The day before we were supposed to go back to school came way too soon. And I couldn't stand it any longer. I either needed to tell him or just give up. Things were still a little odd, and I couldn't figure out what it all meant; I couldn't trust it because I wanted it too much—the touches, the looks, that hug at midnight. They were driving me crazy. Did he know what he was doing? But there was a feeling of something there, something more. God, I was such an idiot.

James came over, like always, and we set up in the living room, like always. But I couldn't sit still; I didn't know what to do. And he could tell something was wrong. He hadn't asked yet, but he would eventually. And then what? What would I say? *Oh by the way, I can talk to ghosts, and I think I'm in love with you.* The thought made me nauseous. Love was a strong word. *Extreme like* might be better. Right. God, I hated me.

"Are you okay?" James was sprawled on one side of the couch, looking at me now, while I was curled up in the other corner. I had no idea what was on TV because I'd lost track, battling my thoughts. Oh, he was talking to me again. "Nate?"

"Um, yeah. I'm fine." I hugged my knees and tried not to look at him. He nodded and turned back to the TV.

It was now or never. *Christ. Here goes nothing.* "Actually—" I cleared my throat. "—there's something I need to talk to you about."

He didn't look nervous, like I would if someone had just said that to me, he looked strangely excited. "What is it?"

I muted the TV, and he turned completely toward me. We were looking at each other over a few feet of couch. Was that too close or too far away? "Um, I don't exactly know how to say this." Resting my chin on my knees, I tried to make myself as small as possible. James's face was kind; he didn't look worried at all. How was he so calm? "It's just, I really trust you, and I hope you won't freak out or anything." Trust. Trust was good. "You remember when we talked about my mom? And you asked why I live here instead of with her and Sarah?"

"Yeah?" *Now* he was starting to look nervous.

I took a deep breath. "Um, it's because of something I can do, that's not exactly normal. My mom couldn't deal with it after my grandmother died, so Aunt Susan took me in."

"So, Susan knows about whatever this 'thing' is you can do?"

"Yeah. It's something that kind of runs in my family and gets passed down generation to generation." He snickered. It sounded like nervous laughter.

"Are you a vampire slayer?"

I gave him a small smile and relaxed just a bit. "No, nothing that cool." I uncoiled and settled back into the couch cushion. "Look, I'm just going to spit it out because you're either going to think I'm crazy or you're not." I closed my eyes. "I can see and talk to ghosts." Silence. I opened my eyes to see him staring at me, mouth hanging open. He closed it with a click.

"You"—he leaned forward—"can *what*?"

He hadn't run away in terror or laughed in my face. That was a good sign.

Sigh. "I can see and talk to ghosts." I shrugged. "It's not something I mean to do; it just happens."

"You're serious right now? This isn't a joke?" He was looking at me skeptically, but there was no fear. "C'mon, Nate. Seriously?"

"I'm serious."

There were several things going on with his face. It was as if he couldn't decide which emotion to land on.

"That is *not* what I thought you were going to say." He moved on quickly before I could respond. "Who do you talk to?" He was choosing belief for the moment, evidently.

"I mostly talk to Nana, my grandmother, because this was her house, and she kind of *sticks* to the location for lack of a better word. That's what they do, you know? Stick to places and people that meant something to them when they were alive."

James went very, very still. "So—" He hesitated. "—they can stick to people?"

Uh-oh. I could guess what he was thinking; that wasn't going to be easy to explain. "Yeah. Yeah, they do." I barely managed to look him in the eye. He believed me, but now he was starting to realize that maybe I could talk to David.

"Is he here right now?"

I flinched at the question and looked past him. Of course, David was here. He was a constant presence. I'd just gotten better at tuning him out. I nodded.

"Prove it." James's eyes narrowed and his jaw clenched. "Go on, prove it."

My mouth went dry. I looked over his shoulder at his dead brother. David thought for a few seconds. "Ask him about Mr. Blue Bear."

"Seriously?" I gaped at David— Was that really what he'd settled on? A toy?

James stood abruptly and whipped around. Following my line of sight, he tried to see who I was talking to. He turned back and looked at me with wide eyes.

David nodded at me.

"Okay, fine." I looked at the floor, not able to look at James. "He says to ask you about Mr. Blue Bear."

"Oh my god." His voice was so shaky. I glanced up to see all the color drain from his face. "Oh my *god*." James swayed. I got up and reached out to steady him, but to my horror, he yanked his arm away. "No. You *knew*. The whole time, you knew. You knew what I was going through, and you didn't say anything. How could you?"

Something in my chest was breaking; it might have been my heart. "James, I—"

"No!" The word was harsh as it cracked between us, and I reflexively took a step back. He swiped at his eyes, scrubbing away angry tears. "I can't believe— You're—You're my— I thought—" His voice broke, and he swallowed hard. "I have to go."

I had to stop him. He had to listen to me. "Wait, please—" I instinctively reached for him.

He looked at me, and I stopped. It was too late. He walked past me, careful not to touch. The glass rattled in the door as it slammed shut.

David looked at me and shrugged. "At least he believed you."

"SHUT UP!" My throat was raw with how loudly I screamed it. "Just shut up!"

"Suit yourself." He faded away as I heard James's car crank and start down the driveway. I'd memorized the sound of his car, realized I'd never hear it here again, and started to cry.

CHAPTER FOURTEEN

I put myself to bed before Aunt Susan got home. It took all of my energy, but I did it. I forgot about the snacks and things still scattered around the living room. It was the DVD menu playing on a loop that brought her to my door. She was still in scrubs and looked exhausted, but her concern must have overridden her need for a shower and sleep.

"Nate?" I pulled my blanket up over my head and heard her sigh. "What happened?" I shook my head, knowing she could see the motion under the blanket. "Oh for god's sake—" The blanket was yanked down before she sat on the edge of the bed. "Tell me what happened."

"I told him."

She sucked in a breath. "I'm guessing it didn't go well?"

I turned on my side, away from her, and talked to the wall. "He believed me, but he'll never forgive me."

"What do you mean?" She went very still. "*Oh.* He's a smart boy." I pulled the blanket back up to my ears, curling myself into a ball. She put a hand on my shoulder. "He'll come around." She was trying really hard to reassure me, but it fell flat. "Won't you see him at school?"

Oh god. *School.*

"I can't go. Aunt Susan, *please* don't make me go." I was pleading with her, and I didn't care. I was shaking from the effort of trying not to cry and tried to curl up tighter to make it stop before she felt it. Too late.

"It's okay. I won't make you go until you're ready." She brushed the hair off my forehead, and I closed my eyes against the sudden hot tears. "Shh. It's okay."

It was really not.

* * *

I spent the next two days in bed. Aunt Susan brought me sandwiches that I didn't eat and stood at the door sighing. I ignored her.

Then, I could swear she sent Arthur in to do her dirty work, because he jumped up on the bed and curled up right beside me. He never did that. If he slept inside, he'd usually take up the couch or go in Aunt Susan's room. But he'd been snuggling the crap out of me for hours. It didn't really help, but I could appreciate the effort.

I picked up my phone again to text James and stopped myself. Again. *Text. Don't text. Text. Don't text.* I threw the phone down to the foot of the bed so I'd have to make an effort to reach it. Arthur raised his head to look at me. I scratched his ears, closed my eyes, and went back to sleep. It was the only thing that helped.

* * *

Nothing. There was nothing. He was never going to talk to me ever again.

* * *

Thursday came, and I made myself get out of bed. I couldn't stay there forever. Aunt Susan seemed surprised, but she didn't say anything as we silently floated around each other getting ready. The drive to school was only filled with the sound of the radio, but she squeezed my shoulder once before I got out of the car. I could feel eyes on me as I walked through the doors. Looking straight ahead, I didn't stop until I got to my seat in homeroom. The chair next to mine was empty, the one that belonged to James, and my stomach hurt.

I looked up in time to see him framed in the doorway. When his eyes met mine, he looked away quickly and walked to another empty desk toward the front of the room. I should have stayed home. It was singularly the most horrible day ever, including the day when my mom had finally told me I had to go and live somewhere else. And when Aunt Susan had stepped forward and told me I was coming home with her, ruining her relationship with her sister forever. This was worse than all of that.

David didn't look very happy either. He'd followed James into the classroom and now leaned against the wall, frowning. He glowed brighter in agitation as he looked between us, saving his sharpest glare for James, who was steadfastly not looking at me. A little twinge of gratitude cut through the despair of being in the same room as James, but it washed away in blink as soon as the bell rang.

I waited until everyone else was gone before moving from my seat. I tried not to watch as James left the room, but my eyes automatically followed him. He didn't look any happier than me, but that didn't help anything.

* * *

I made it through Calculus and part of the way through Chemistry before exploiting Mr. Gardener's soft spot for me and making my escape to the restroom. I'd only managed some juice and toast that morning for which I was profoundly grateful, because it made an immediate reappearance as soon as I threw myself into a stall. The edge of the seat was blessedly cool against my forehead.

I couldn't do this.

I flushed and dragged myself up to the sink to splash some cold water on my face. After rinsing my mouth out a few times, I leaned against the wall and considered what to do. Aunt Susan wouldn't have left for her shift yet, but it would definitely make her late if she had to come get me. I hated to do it, but I couldn't stay here.

Can you come get me? I'm sorry.

Her reply was immediate.

Don't be sorry. On my way.

Thank god. I went to the school nurse—thankfully, I'd grabbed my bag before fleeing the classroom—and she sent a message to Mr. Gardener. I then sat with a cool cloth on my forehead, waiting until Aunt Susan got there.

She took one look at me as I walked toward her, and her face fell. "Oh, sweetie." She went silent when I shook my head, falling into step beside me as we made our way to the car. She was already dressed in scrubs for work, which, of course, just made me feel worse. We got in the car and rode in silence for a bit.

"I'm sorry. I threw up."

I put my head against the window, looking at the world passing us by. She didn't say anything, only took my hand and squeezed it once before putting her hand back on the wheel.

* * *

Aunt Susan stuck around until I finally told her I'd be fine. I just needed to go to bed. She paused at the door, keys in her hand. "Text me if you need me. I'll keep my phone with me."

I nodded, and she finally left. I dragged myself to the bathroom and brushed my teeth before changing back into my pajamas and burying myself in bed. Arthur jumped up beside me to take up his caretaker role, and I stared at the ceiling until exhaustion forced me to sleep.

* * *

The next day, Aunt Susan checked on me before she left for work, but I honestly couldn't have said when that was. The TV was on though I'd hit mute because I couldn't stand the noise.

I was empty.

Aunt Susan had convinced me to leave my room, but I only did because I was tired of Nana's worried face. She'd shown up in the middle of the night when I was up and hadn't left me alone since. I'd promised to join the rest of the world, which apparently just meant the other rooms of the house, and that was enough to get her to go away for a while.

So I was on the couch. I hated it. Thank god Aunt Susan hadn't suggested going back to school again; I didn't think I could bear it. James ignoring me was worse than I could have ever imagined.

How could I have been so stupid? I should have known better by now. James couldn't accept it; he never would. The betrayal in his eyes when he'd put the pieces together was shattering. I'd never seen anyone that angry before.

To make things worse, Sarah emailed me. We didn't text because she didn't want Mom to know she was in contact with me. But the school email was pretty safe; Mom would never check that.

To: nshaw@mountainviewhs.edu
From: sshaw@mountainviewhs.edu

Are you okay?
Sarah

Great. I blew out a breath and typed out an answer.

To: sshaw@mountainviewhs.edu
From: nshaw@mountainviewhs.edu

Not really. Don't really want to talk about it.
Nate.

To: nshaw@mountainviewhs.edu
From: sshaw@mountainviewhs.edu

I talked to James. Well, he emailed me first. What happened with you two?
Sarah

That got my attention. Why would James contact Sarah? Were they talking about me behind my back? No.

To: sshaw@mountainviewhs.edu
From: nshaw@mountainviewhs.edu

He's not speaking to me right now. What did he say?
Nate

To: nshaw@mountainviewhs.edu
From: sshaw@mountainviewhs.edu

He wanted to make sure you were okay. I may have given him a hard time.
Sarah

That got the first hint of a smile from me in days. I could only imagine what she'd said. Did that mean he was worried about me? Did he even care?

To: sshaw@mountainviewhs.edu
From: nshaw@mountainviewhs.edu

I told him about that thing I do. He freaked out. I haven't talked to him in almost a week. Don't give him too hard a time. It's not his fault. And stop talking about me behind my back.
Nate

I closed my email because I didn't want to talk about it anymore. Hopefully, the weekend would be a little better.

Yeah. I didn't think so either.

* * *

I actually showered but only because Aunt Susan took one look at my greasy hair and shoved me into the bathroom with a towel and a pair of underwear before she left for her shift. Then I felt bad because that meant she'd also been doing all the laundry. And the cycle of despair continued. I was in pajamas again, but at least I was clean.

This detail was important, because suddenly someone was knocking loudly on the door. Not just knocking but pounding on the back door hard enough to rattle the glass. I peeked out the window over the kitchen sink, and my heart stopped. James's car was sitting in the driveway, shadowed by the fading light.

I took a deep breath and yanked the door open before he could start pounding on it again. His eyes met mine for a split second as he hesitated for a moment, uncertainty on his face, and then he pushed past me into the house. He looked awful. I quietly closed the door and watched as he paced back and forth in the kitchen before leaning on the table, head bowed. Neither one of us had said a word.

He looked up at me, and I couldn't read his face at all. He opened his mouth, closed it, and shook his head. I wanted to tell him to just spit it out, but I didn't have the right to demand anything of him right then. It was my fault we were in such a mess; I was lucky he was here at all.

"Is Susan here?" I blinked at him for a few seconds before it registered what he was asking.

"No, um, she's at work." It came out as more of a croak. I cleared my throat. "James, I'm sorry—"

"Don't." His hands were clenched into fists. "I'm the one who should be apologizing."

What? I leaned against the counter to stay upright. "I don't understand." My voice shook, and I cleared my throat again. I was inexplicably thirsty and couldn't help but notice he was wearing the shirt I'd gotten him for Christmas. "James, why are you here?" He flinched at the question, and I immediately felt bad.

"I missed you." His voice cracked.

"What?"

His eyes were fixed on the tabletop. "I missed you."

"Oh. I missed you, too." *So much,* I wanted to say. *So much.*

He finally raised his head and looked at me, his eyes red-rimmed and exhausted. We were standing a few feet apart. It felt like miles.

His jaw was clenched; it looked like he was warring with himself about something. He was going to leave. He'd said what he needed to say, and now he was leaving. My gaze on the patch of floor between us, I waited for the sound of the door closing. A few footsteps, and he was standing right in front of me, closer than usual. I looked up, surprised, and his face was soft, questioning. I didn't know the answer. I didn't even know the question.

The silence dragged out between us.

James moved suddenly, stepping closer. I didn't have time to react before his lips were on mine, soft and dry and warm. I drew in a sharp breath through my nose, too stunned to move. He pulled back, looking terrified. "I'm sorry, Nate. I—"

I got a handful of T-shirt and pulled him back in, kissing him, noses bumping awkwardly, *no idea* what I was doing. *He's kissing me, he's kissing me, he's kissing—*When he slid a hand into my hair, my skin felt like it was on fire. I couldn't let go of his shirt. My hand was trapped between us, and his heart was racing beneath my palm.

If I hadn't been leaning against the counter, I'd have slid to the floor when the hand in my hair tilted my head just so, and—*Oh.* I was lost in an eternity of sliding lips before James pulled away, resting his forehead against mine.

"Okay?" His voice was low, and all I could do was nod. I'd somehow wound my arms around him, clutching two handfuls of the back of his T-shirt. His fingers were still buried in my hair, but his other hand was on my hip, his thumb rubbing circles on the skin just above the waistband of my pajama pants. That was very, very distracting.

I loosened my death grip on his shirt and flattened my palms on his back, trying to catch my breath. *Oh god.* "Um—" Yes, very articulate. His breath was soft on my cheek, and I closed my eyes. I tightened my arms around him and pressed my face into his neck, breathing him in.

The giggles came out of nowhere. His arms tightened around me while I laughed out the rush of emotion and exhaustion of the past few days. I quieted eventually. After wiping my streaming eyes, I lay my hand flat on James's chest again, touching him because I could. He cupped the back of my neck and brushed his lips against my temple.

"Are you okay?"

I looked up into his eyes. Concern was written clearly across his face. When I nodded, he pulled me close again. There were things to talk about, whether we liked it or not, but I wanted to stay like this forever. He tilted my head up and kissed me again. It was so very hard not to think about how much more experienced he was. It wasn't jealousy, not really. It was the fact that I wasn't the first person he'd ever kissed. Shaking it off, I sank into the kiss. A swipe of his tongue on my lower lip made it almost too much.

I broke off with a gasp. "We really need to talk." He nodded, glasses adorably askew. But then I went against my words, and it was my turn to pull him in. He grinned against my lips. It was addictive: his mouth, his *oh god tongue*, and— Yep. Time to stop before things got embarrassing. I gently pushed him back and suddenly realized exactly how thin my pajama pants really were. My face went bright red; it couldn't be helped.

He straightened his glasses and slid his palm down my arm to take my hand in his. "You're right, we do need to talk. In here?" He tipped his head toward the living room before leading me, fingers laced with mine, to the couch. The couch where we'd had so many good times. Where I'd learned what it was to have a friend. Where I'd confessed things he'd accepted and things he hadn't. The hurt returned in a rush, making me sit like I had that day, knees pulled up, defensive and tense.

James was sitting on the other end; the same space between us as just a few days ago. He gripped his hands in his lap, staring at them intently. "First of all, I want to say I'm sorry for how I acted. You caught me by surprise and—" He broke off, shaking his head. "Screw that. I was an asshole. You trusted me with something pretty huge, and I overreacted." He looked up, eyes searching. "I hated not being around you at school. I'm really sorry for all of it."

I blinked in surprise and took in a huge breath, easing the tightness in my chest. I shrugged. "It's okay. At least you came back."

He scooted across that space between us, looking at me as if asking permission. "I shouldn't have left like I did." He reached to cup my cheek, running a thumb under one eye. "You look exhausted. I'm sorry."

"Stop apologizing." I couldn't help but lean into that touch. It was like I'd been freezing and needed to soak up every bit of warmth I could. "You don't look much better." And he really didn't. He had dark circles to match mine, and he looked drained.

He snorted, nodding. "You're right." He took my hand again and turned so that he was sitting next to me. "I should probably go home."

"Stay." It came out in a rush before I knew what I was going to say. "I mean, go if you want to." I uncurled, and now we were sitting side by side, fingers laced between us. I squeezed his hand. "What about, um, this?"

I was trying very hard not to be nervous, but there it was. I mean, logically, he was the one who'd come back. *He'd kissed me.* He was sitting here holding my hand in my living room after *kissing me in my kitchen.* I was still nervous.

"Well—" He stared at our hands like he wasn't quite sure how that had happened either. "What do you want?"

What did I want? To stay right here like that for the rest of my life? My head was starting to hurt from a combination of too much and too little sleep. Sleeping because you couldn't bear to drag yourself out of bed didn't count.

"I want—" I coughed, trying to move the lump that had suddenly appeared in my throat. "—I want this." I lifted our interlocked hands, turning them over so mine was on top. Looked at them again and tried not to sound too idiotic. "It's just that I— I've never—"

James leaned over and kissed my cheek. "Yeah. Don't worry about it. We'll figure it out together, because I want to give this a try, too." The mood was broken when a huge yawn escaped me, and James laughed. "You need to go to bed."

I yawned again. "So do you." I picked at a thread at the hem of my T-shirt. "Are you going to, um, stay?" I yanked on the thread, breaking it.

"Sure." He stood, pulling me up after him. He led me into my bedroom, and when he let go of my hand, I missed it immediately. But that part was comfortable. That part we'd done so many times. He knew exactly which drawer the jogging pants he usually borrowed were in. "I'll be right back."

He went to change in the bathroom, and I started to panic. Just a little bit.

I automatically started setting up the air mattress that lived in my room now, but stopped mid-action. If we were doing *this*, then what did it mean? I looked at my double bed, and it seemed tiny even though I had plenty of room to starfish out in the middle of it. *Oh god, what did he expect?* He was so much more experienced, and he'd had actual relationships and everything. A sudden realization brought all of my whirling thoughts to a screeching halt.

Has he had sex?

Oh my god, I bet he has. *Stop thinking about it; stop thinking about it. It'll be fine.* Everything would be fine. He knew I'd never, well, anything, so it'd be okay.

I must have spent more time than I realized freaking out because suddenly James was right there beside me, wearing borrowed pajamas and everything. I absolutely did not make a mortifying squeak of surprise. "Hi. Um."

He paused midway through putting his stuff on top of my dresser to glance at me; I guess I had an odd look on my face. There was that insane urge to giggle again. I tried to tamp it down; at least some form of maturity was needed here.

James finally turned and lay a hand on each of my shoulders, guaranteeing my full attention. "You're freaking out."

"Am not." So much for maturity.

He snorted. "You so are." He gestured toward the bed. "You're going to bed. If you want, I can sleep there with you. Just sleep, okay?" His face was serious now. "If that makes you uncomfortable in any way, I can use the air mattress. No problem, no hard feelings. Okay?"

I blew out a breath and tried to calm down. Of course he would be understanding and sweet. No big deal. It was no big deal.

"Okay. Right." I pulled back the comforter and sheet and slid into bed, moving over as close to the wall as I could get. James put his glasses on the nightstand and climbed in, his shoulder pressing tightly against mine. Awkward. I lay there staring at the ceiling. Again. It was like I'd forgotten how to sleep. When James breathed out a sigh beside me, I was convinced he was going to get up and give up entirely on me.

"Do you trust me?" His voice was gentle.

What? "Of course I do. Why?"

"Turn on your side, toward the wall. No, wait. You don't like being boxed in. Get up for a second." He got up, waited for me to do the same, and then scooted back under the covers, his back to the wall. I understood immediately and gingerly climbed in, lying on my side, facing the room.

There were still several inches between us. I just went for it, pushing back until we were flush together. James snaked an arm around me, pulling me closer. It was warm and calming as the tension from the last few days drained from my body. My eyes closed for a second before I realized what he had said. "How did you know?"

"Hmm. Know what?" He already sounded half-asleep.

I twisted my head towards him but couldn't really see him. "That I don't like being closed in." I felt him shrug before he pressed a kiss to the back my neck that tingled all the way down to my toes.

"Dunno. Just noticed is all." He yawned, fading fast.

I snuggled, yes *snuggled*, back into his body, stifling a yawn. "Thank you."

Another kiss, to my ear that time, and we fell asleep.

CHAPTER FIFTEEN

Things I noticed immediately when I woke up: I was warm and comfortable and it felt like I'd been sleeping for years. Also, I really, really needed to pee. It took me a few seconds to remember what the weight draped across me was. I carefully moved James's arm to slide out of bed, only to look up at Aunt Susan, coffee mug in hand, leaning in the doorway. Her eyebrows were trying to crawl up into her hairline, and I put a finger to my lips to keep her from saying anything until we got out of my room.

She gave me until we got into the kitchen before letting loose. "What the hell?" It was hard to tell from her expression if she was mad or upset or impressed or what. "Seriously, what happened last night?"

My face flushed hot as she narrowed her eyes at me. It was way too early for this conversation. I glanced at the clock. *Oups.* It was still too early for this conversation, at least until I went to the bathroom. I was on the verge of dancing like a toddler.

"Hold that thought." I held up a finger, ignoring her protests as I quickly went to take care of business, which included carefully brushing my teeth. A quick glance in my room to check on James, still asleep in my bed, but I dared not linger at the door. Aunt Susan would come drag me back by the ear if I wasn't careful. She was still giving me a narrow-eyed glare over her mug when I returned to the kitchen. I took a seat at the table and threw myself upon her mercy. "Okay. Go."

She sat her mug down on the counter and folded her arms across her chest. She started to say something and stopped, brow furrowing, and then tried again. "Okay, let me get this straight." I tried not to snicker. Maturity. Yes. Her glare intensified. "When I left to go to work, you were the saddest puddle of pining I'd ever seen in my life." I started to defend myself, and she shushed me with a look. "Yes. You were. Don't interrupt. Anyway, I look in on you because I am *worried about you* and find you cuddled up in bed with James. So—" She folded her hands on the table. "—why don't you tell me what the hell is going on."

I'd evidently lost all control of my face because I broke out in what had to be the goofiest grin, making her eyes widen in response. "He, um, came over last night and apologized."

"Apologized, huh. Is that what you call it now?"

"Aunt Susan!"

She waved her mug at me. "What am I supposed to think? Were you careful?"

I gave her a blank look until it dawned on me what she was talking about. I covered my face with my hands. "Oh my god. Nothing happened. Well, he apologized, and then he kissed me." The giddiness was back for a moment before the mortification took over again. "But nothing else happened. We slept. That's it. Jesus Christ, I am not doing this without coffee." I got up, chair scraping back, and stalked over to the coffee pot. It was empty. "Why? Why would you do this to me?"

She shrugged. "Maybe if you hadn't been sleeping in late with your *boyfriend*, you might have gotten coffee." I looked at her and caught her grinning behind her mug. "I'm happy for you, but don't think you're getting out of the full safe sex talk. I'm serious."

I wanted to sink through the floor. "You are the worst aunt ever."

"I love you, too." She opened a cabinet and pulled out our seldom-used carafe, obviously full of coffee, and poured herself another cup. "I'm just going to go and hide in my room for a while so that you don't spontaneously combust from embarrassment." She reached up and gave my hair a ruffle for good measure before going to her room.

"Is she gone?"

I'd been so lost in thought while sipping my coffee I didn't hear James come into the kitchen. He'd spoken right by my ear and had to put a hand on my arm when I jumped.

"Sorry." He wound his arms around my waist and propped his chin on my shoulder. "I've wanted to do this for a while."

"Really?" I covered one his hands with mine and enjoyed the closeness. "Why didn't you?"

I felt him shrug. "Honestly, I don't know. I mean, I thought there was something there but..."

"You didn't want to scare me off?" His breath on my neck made me shiver. He kissed the same place, and there was that tingle again. *Holy hell.*

"Something like that. I mean, I like you. A lot. You know that, right?" I nodded, not really able to concentrate on an intelligent response. I needed to get a handle on things. Seriously.

I could think again when he pulled away. "Coffee?"

He shook his head and got out the orange juice instead. He was definitely not the caffeine junkie I was. I opened the pantry to check on our cereal selections when I felt tentative fingers on my elbow, plucking at the hem of my shirtsleeve. I turned and James gave me an uncertain smile. *Oh. Should I instigate or wait for him? Screw it.*

I put a hand on his upper arm—firm and warm under the sleeve of his T-shirt—to pull him closer. He stepped toward me easily, but he must have sensed my hesitation because his smile widened a bit as he waited for me to make a move. I closed my eyes as I leaned in and brushed his lips with mine. It was like that first kiss all over again. His fingers were in my hair again, and the kiss intensified. I crowded him against the counter—he tasted like orange juice—and suddenly his chest was pressed against mine.

His hands were splayed on my back, warm palms and fingers pressing me closer, closer. I was still gripping his arms, holding on tightly, as my knees would buckle otherwise. A brush of tongue on my lower lip, and I was just going with it. I'd never felt anything like that, never felt so close to another person.

Of course, it was at that point that I heard a throat being cleared very loudly. I pulled away from James so quickly I almost lost my balance, which would have just added to the embarrassment. Aunt Susan was standing in the kitchen doorway, and her smug smile could have been seen from outer space. She was trying very hard to look stern and adult, but it was obvious she was fighting a huge grin at catching me making out with my—I had no idea what he was—person, best friend, *boyfriend*? Putting that away for the moment. My face was on fire.

"Morning, boys." She walked to the coffee pot, giving us a moment to get ourselves together. "Don't mind me."

I chanced a look at James. It was gratifying in a weird way to see a hint of pink to his cheeks as well. He caught my eye and gave me a silly grin that made me want to kiss him all over again. *Shelving that thought.* I ran a hand through my hair, trying to get it to do something other than stick up everywhere, but it was futile. And to be fair, James looked pretty ruffled, too. It was a good look on him. I cleared my throat and gave Aunt Susan my attention.

"Um, morning?"

She smirked at me, raising an eyebrow. I rolled my eyes and continued getting things out for breakfast. I was suddenly starving.

* * *

Because Aunt Susan was a horrible, horrible person, she joined us for breakfast. We sat at the kitchen table, a weird but not entirely uncomfortable silence between us. James and I ate without looking at each other, and Aunt Susan watched us not looking at each other, smiling into her coffee. She finally decided to break the standoff.

"Okay, boys." She sat her mug on the table and crossed her arms. Pausing mid-bite, I put my fork back down on my plate. She smiled at us. "First of all, I just want to say I am very happy you've figured yourselves out. Mostly for my own sanity. I mean, *seriously*." I took a deep breath, not exactly sure what she was getting at, just as James made an odd choked sound. He carefully sat his juice glass back on the table and turned his attention to her. "And I just want you to know"— she looked both of us in the eye in turn—"that I am saying this out of love for both of you. If you have any questions"—another stern look—"and I mean, *any* questions, you can come to me. Okay?"

I nodded quickly, and James did the same. That wasn't too terrible, I suppose. I mean, she was a medical professional; we'd talked about *stuff* before. In fact, I thought she was being pretty cool about the whole thing.

"If you're done, Nate. I'd like to speak to James alone for a minute."

Never mind, not cool at all! Red alert! Red alert!

"What? Why?" My voice was high with panic. James looked at me for the first time since we sat down, eyes wide. Aunt Susan rolled her eyes.

"Oh for the love of— I'm not going to *do* anything to him; I just want to have a chat." She looked at me innocently, and I had a strong feeling about exactly what kind of chat she was talking about. James glanced at her. My guess was he knew, too. He sighed and tipped his head toward the living room.

"Go on. It'll be fine." He gave me a weak grin. "Promise."

I stood, giving Aunt Susan a pleading look that she shooed away, and squeezed James's shoulder because I just couldn't help myself. As I dragged myself to the living room, I wondered if it would be possible to eavesdrop without her knowing.

"If you try to listen in, I will send you to your room; I swear to god."

Guess not, then. Throwing myself onto the couch, I pointedly turned on the TV so she could get on with it. I was fairly certain she was giving him the "Hurt him and answer to me" speech. Hopefully, after everything else that had happened, this wouldn't scare him off.

I was flipping through channels when David appeared on the couch beside me. Since I was kind of expecting him, I didn't jump. Much.

"Told you."

I rolled my eyes. Of course he would show up just to gloat. Fine, I'd give him this one. Plus, it was a distraction from whatever was happening in the kitchen.

"Yes. You were right." I kept my voice low, though they couldn't hear me. "Happy?"

He wasn't grinning in triumph like I expected. He seemed quite serious. "You have no idea." Looking at his hands, he held them up to see the flicker of the TV screen through them. I waited for him to continue, not entirely sure what that change meant. "Will I always be here?"

I blinked at the odd question. I suppose it wasn't that odd when you thought about it. "I don't know."

He sighed. "Promise me, if I'm not here to watch over him, that you'll take care of him." He turned to look at me, dropping his hands. "I told you he's slow on the uptake. So try not to hurt him?" He laughed to himself. "I don't think you ever would, though."

"Not on purpose."

"Good." He nodded. "Good." He glanced toward the kitchen and started to fade. "He's coming this way. Talk to you later."

I just had time to nod before James appeared in the doorway. He was smiling, so it must not have been that terrifying. He dropped onto the couch beside me, sitting closer than usual, pressing against me from shoulder to thigh. "I'm still alive. She's not that scary."

I snorted. "You're on her good side right now, just wait." His hand was on my knee, and I lost my train of thought for a second. "Um"—staring at his hand—"what did she say?"

"You know, the usual. Hurt him and you're a dead man." He took his hand from my knee and turned to look me in the eye. "I'm sorry I was such an idiot." And now I was wondering what else she said to him.

"I, um—" I was at a loss for words because he *had* hurt me, mostly without meaning to, and I wasn't sure if I should tell him or if it would just make me seem sad. There was something I had to know. "If this is too much— If what I can do is too much, tell me now, okay?" That was his out, his chance to take it all back. It was suddenly far more serious than I originally meant it to be, but I had to say it. "Don't let me have, I mean, don't— Just don't." Stupid emotion was getting the best of me. God, I was ruining this, and we'd been together in whatever we had going between us for less than twenty-four hours.

"God. Come here." He grabbed my hand and pulled me with him as he lay back on the couch. I ended up with my head on his chest, somehow, and his hand in my hair. His shirt was soft under my cheek, and I could hear his heartbeat. "It's not too much. It's weird and unusual, but it's who you are. Okay?"

I nodded against him, feeling a little bit better. It was going to be fine.

* * *

James got the remote without making me move, and we lay there bickering over what to watch just like we always did, except now we were stretched out together on the couch. I was a little squished, but you couldn't have paid me to move. He finally settled on a bad sci-fi movie, that I was sure I'd seen before, and moved the remote out of my reach. He was grinning when he smacked my hand away,

"You're not even going to watch it, so what does it matter?"

I gaped at him and sputtered. "It's the principle of the thing! It's *so* bad!"

He laughed, and I sat up a bit and acted like I was going to shove him off the couch. He caught my hand in his and leaned in to kiss me, still smiling.

That was...different. And it made me very glad Aunt Susan had already left for a rare weekend shift. I was draped across his chest, feeling like my bones were turning into goo. I pulled away with a gasp because I'd forgotten to breathe. He was breathing hard, too. I buried my face in his neck; I didn't know what else to do.

"You okay?" His voice was full of concern.

I shook my head slightly and shifted my hips away from him as much as I could. My body was more than willing, while my brain was yelling at me to slow down a freaking minute. At least he seemed to be in the same state. *God.*

"Sorry." My voice cracked. I took a deep breath, pulling my flushed face away from my hiding place against his neck. "Sorry, I—"

He kissed my forehead, and I could feel his smile against my skin. "Too fast?"

"Yeah. I just—" I scooted back a bit so I could see him. Blowing out a breath, I gave him a grin. "Yeah. Too fast."

He wrapped his arm around my shoulders and pulled me back into the position I was laying in earlier. I sank into the comfort again. He sighed. "We can take things as slowly as you want, you know."

"Yeah." He would never pressure me into anything, but now I had a whole new set of things to worry about. I had to ask him. I couldn't help myself; I had to know. "Um, have you ever, you know?"

He was very quiet, and I wished I could unask the question. Of course he had. He'd had *relationships*. Until last night, I'd never even kissed anyone. Why was I such an idiot?

"Stop it." His voice was low, and he pressed a kiss to my forehead. "You can ask me anything, you know." He was silent for another minute or two. "Twice."

Twice. He'd...twice. I tried not to tense up. I mean, I shouldn't be freaking out, I'd asked the question after all. I shouldn't have asked if I didn't really want to know. Twice.

A horrible thought hit me like a freight train. "Who with?"

Not with her, not with her, please for the love of god, not with freaking Margaret Kennemer. Please...

"No one you know." I let out the breath I was holding. *Thank god.* He chuckled and buried his nose in my hair. "It was back in Cincinnati. There was a girl I went out with a few times and then Matthew once before we broke up."

"Why did you break up?" The floodgates had opened apparently, and now I wanted to know *everything*.

He huffed out a breath that tickled my ear and made me squirm. "After David, you know, I was a mess. And then we moved here."

"Oh." That hadn't occurred to me. It really, really should have.

"It wasn't anything serious." His hand slid up my back, and then his fingers were in my hair again. I didn't want to move from this spot ever again.

Remember how I said I couldn't recall the last time I'd been properly hugged? That was what I needed, but I'd had no idea. My eyelids started to droop again, and I made an embarrassing noise of contentment.

"Go to sleep." His voice was soft.

* * *

We stayed on the couch together for a while, curled together comfortably, and I dozed on and off. The stress of the last few days wasn't going to be washed away by one good night's rest. I didn't dream. I also hadn't dreamed the night before with James's arm wrapped around me and his chest pressed to my back. It'd been the first bit of sleep I'd gotten in days that didn't have me gasping awake, with some unknown dreaded *thing* breathing down my neck.

I jerked awake after some time, completely forgetting where I was for a moment. James's arms tightened around me before I could knock us both off the couch.

"You're okay." His voice was right in my ear, and I realized I was clutching his T-shirt like a lifeline. "You're okay."

"Let me up." I needed space. He stood up, and I made my way clumsily to my feet. "Sorry."

"Don't worry about it." He stretched. Okay, ogling the strip of stomach that showed under the hem of his T-shirt was totally fine now. So I did. He saw me looking and grinned. "Want to go and get some dinner? We could go to that burger place again."

A surprised laugh escaped my mouth. "Like a date?"

He shrugged and gave me a shy look. "Sure. Why not?"

"Okay." I was smiling like an idiot, but what could I say? I was happy. I picked at my pajama pants. "Maybe we should get dressed?"

He grabbed his jeans and changed in the bathroom while I quickly got ready in my bedroom. I looked in the mirror hanging over my dresser and tried to smooth down my hair before finally giving up. It looked like I'd been sleeping on someone for the past few hours. I felt...giddy. Those butterflies were working overtime.

And of course, that was when David decided to show up again. Followed quickly by Nana. It was like they were starting to plan these things, I swear to god.

I had never seen ghosts look so freaking smug. "Stop right there. Yes, I know what you're both going to say. No, I don't want to hear it. I'm very sorry, Nana, for being so blunt, but I don't want to make a big deal out of this. Okay?"

I looked at both of them with as much sternness as I could come up with at the moment. They both nodded. And I gave them a curt nod back.

"And no more hanging around, got it?" My face flushed, but I needed to lay down some ground rules. Boundaries, even. They both nodded again. I heard James moving around so I only had seconds before he came back to see if I was ready. "I love you, Nana. Now, shoo." I'd just shooed my Nana away. I could only hope she was so happy about what had happened that she would forgive me. David would get over it.

James walked in as they winked out of sight.

"Ready?"

I grabbed my wallet and phone and shoved them into my jeans pockets. "Sure. Let's go."

It really wasn't like that first time we'd gone to the movies together, though. That time, it wasn't a date.

Chapter Sixteen

I didn't know what I expected. Whatever it was, it couldn't compare. It was like any other time we'd gone to town, but this time, he held my hand in the car. His thumb running over my knuckles made it very hard to pay attention to our conversation, but I managed.

James chuckled. "You remember the first time we went to the movies?" He glanced at me sideways. "I wanted to kiss you then, when I dropped you off."

"Really?" It was nice to know I hadn't completely misread that. There was no way I would have done anything about it, but it was still nice to know. "Why didn't you?"

"I wasn't sure how you'd react. I mean, it's hard to read sometimes, you know?" He gave my fingers a quick squeeze before turning the wheel to park. When we got out of the car, it hit me that, as accepting as most people were, this was still a small town. It didn't help that I was an outsider at school or that Penny had been trying to make a move on James since he'd broken up with Margo. What was she going to say when she saw us together like this? How would people react to us together?

Taking a deep breath, I stopped James with a hand to his shoulder before we went into the restaurant. "Look—" I took my hand away because was *that* okay? "I'm following your lead here with—" I gestured between the two of us. "—this. Okay?" I laughed nervously and ran a hand through my hair. "I'm just a little out of my depth here."

"You really *are* nervous." James grinned at me as he turned to the door and pulled it open, waving me inside. "You'll be fine, trust me. It'll be like any other time, I promise."

We got a table, and he was right. It *was* just like any other time we'd done this, but when his knee bumped mine, he left it there instead of moving away. It was nice. I didn't feel so self-conscious leaning in to listen to what he was saying and making eye contact felt natural instead of something I had to hide. Even seeing Penny didn't rattle me. She glared but didn't engage, thank god.

* * *

We were almost finished with our food when James finally asked something I knew he'd been putting off ever since I put him off the first time.

"I'm sorry, but I have to ask; what happened with Penny? You didn't want to tell me before because it has to do with—" He waved a fry in the air. "—*that*, but can you tell me now?"

I had to tell him. No, I *needed* to tell him. She was the one that we were going to have to worry about the most, and he deserved to know. It sounded kind of dumb when I thought about it. I finished chewing to buy some time to go over what I wanted to say.

"It's okay. You need to know, and honestly, I've never been able to tell anyone about it before." I thought for a second more. "Well, anyone living."

I was relieved when he smiled. I was afraid of saying the wrong thing, joking about something that was so serious just a few short days ago. I had to trust him. But it was like he could read my mind.

"It's fine. Go on."

I took a drink of my shake, barely tasting it, stalling. *Fine.* "It's kind of dumb, really. Penny and I were friends through middle school." He made a surprised noise. "Yeah, right? Anyway, I was first able to do what I do when I was twelve. I was lucky enough to have my Nana around, but that was when she was first starting to get sick." I stopped and took another drink. I didn't like thinking about that time. "She was able to talk me through a lot of it, but when she didn't feel well, it was like, they needed someone to talk to, and I was fresh blood."

James put a hand on mine, and I blinked at both of our hands together like that. It helped. "Are you sure you want to talk about this?"

I realized that I really did. I wanted to get all of it out of me so I could get past this mess, take the first step in moving past who I was before. I wasn't alone anymore.

I nodded. "I'm sure." I squeezed his fingers, and he sat back again, waiting for me to continue. "So, it was like an overload, you know? I was able to hide it pretty well to begin with. But then, my mom noticed. That was bad. I could tell she'd heard me talking to them, and she changed. She didn't seem mad or anything, but she wouldn't be in the same room with me. She'd just get a weird look on her face and then make an excuse to go somewhere else. Once I realized what she was doing, it hurt. I spent more and more time with Nana, but it finally got to the point where that couldn't be an option. She was in and out of the hospital, and that is definitely a place I try to avoid at all costs."

"I can understand that."

He was so calm. Despite the seriousness of what we were talking about, it made me want to smile. He *did* understand. I couldn't begin to describe how that felt.

"Yeah." I ran a hand through my hair again, making it worse, but I didn't care. "That went on for a while—my mom avoiding me and me trying to ignore all of the *stuff* coming out of the woodwork.

"I'd just started high school when I'd finally had enough of all of it. There was one of *them* there, you know? He was the janitor years ago, and he loved the school, so he just stayed. He was so happy to have someone to talk to that he surprised the hell out me one day in the library. And of course, the only person that was there to witness me trying to convince *no one* to go away and leave me alone was—"

"Penny." James was nodding along like he could see where the story was going. "What did she do?"

"I tried to talk to her at first. Like I said, we were friends. But she was mad at me. We'd been at a party the weekend before—I can't remember who's now; I don't think I even knew them that well—and she'd tried to kiss me."

James laughed out loud. "And you wouldn't do it."

"Of course not. I was still kind of working things out then, but I definitely didn't want to kiss her. Boy, was she pissed. She refused to talk to me. Then, when she saw what she saw, well—" I shrugged. "You pretty much know the rest."

He was silent for a moment. "So you're telling me that Penny Applegate, most popular girl in school, is still holding a grudge because you wouldn't kiss her when you were, what, thirteen?"

I nodded, trying to keep a solemn look, but the grin was trying so hard to escape. He laughed. Loud enough that people looked at him a little funny. The grin won, and then I was laughing too, harder than I had in a long time.

James got control of himself and picked up his milkshake in a toast. "Here's to not kissing Penny Applegate."

I knocked my milkshake against his. "I'll drink to that."

* * *

The drive back was quiet, only filled by the low music from the radio. James was clearly working over something in his head, and I wondered if I should ask or wait for him to spit it out. He'd reached his hand out for mine once we'd started back and hadn't let go of it since. He started to speak and stopped himself. And then again.

"Nate?"

He sounded so unsure, I was afraid of what he was going to say. He must have picked up on that because he squeezed my hand. I cleared my throat and hoped my palm wouldn't get sweaty.

"Yeah?"

"Is David here now?" The question took me by surprise. The glimmer of David's form shone as he leaned forward inserting himself between the car seats. *Great.* God, he was annoying.

I debated for another moment, and James glanced over at me as the silence drew out. It was best to go with the truth. "Yes."

The car jerked, making James let go of my hand.

"Sorry, sorry."

His knuckles were white on the steering wheel, and he let out a nervous laugh. "I guess I shouldn't have asked if I didn't really want to know."

He deserved to know; that is exactly why he'd asked. "Pull over." I pointed to the tiny gas station that everyone went to on this side of town. "Right up here. You shouldn't be driving for this."

He eased the car into the parking lot and killed the engine, the sudden silence dragging on for a split second before he took a deep breath and gave me a shaky smile.

"I'm okay." I gave him a pointed look, and he rolled his eyes. "Really."

I needed to help things along. It was only fair. "What do you want to know?"

"Where is he?"

David had moved back a bit, but with James's question, he pressed forward so far that he would have been blocking James from my sight if he'd been solid. It was a little eerie seeing James through him, so I gave a quick jerk of my head to tell him to back off already. At the motion, James turned toward the back seat, scanning the empty space.

"Back there?"

"Kind of." Talking about David wasn't going to be easy no matter how good James was being about it. James was still looking at the back seat as if he'd be able to see David. "He keeps leaning forward and getting in my way." I gave James a small smile. "He's kind of a pain in the ass." I had to have a sense of humor about this.

"Oh."

James drew back, bumping his elbow on the door. Okay, no more trying to be funny.

I offered him my hand, and he took it. I didn't want him to be afraid, but he needed this. "Do you have anything you want to ask him?" I thought for a second. Maybe I was going about this the wrong way. "David, do you have anything you want to say?"

David moved into my line of sight again, and goosebumps ran up my arm where he had gotten too close. I rolled my eyes, trying to pretend it was the most normal thing in the world.

When I said "Back off," James squeezed my hand hard.

"Fine." David backed up just enough so that he wasn't close enough to physically affect me anymore. "Ask him—ask him if he's okay now. If he's going to be okay."

It was what I expected, but strangely sweet coming from him.

"James?" He was still staring at the back seat, craning his neck to peek over the edge of the front seat. He looked at me with wide eyes. "You're sure you want to do this?"

"Yeah." He shifted uncomfortably, eyes darting around the car. "What did he say?"

I smiled at him. "He wants to make sure that you are going to be okay now."

The tension in his body came down a notch. "Really?"

"Yeah. You okay?" James nodded and looked a little less wide-eyed. "You can talk to him, if you want to."

"Okay." He turned and faced me, still giving little glances to the back seat. "Um. Yeah. I'm okay now. I think." He still had a good grip on my hand, and I squeezed his fingers encouragingly. He looked me in the eye. "So that's, um, yeah. I'm *going* to be okay."

I turned toward David who was smiling now. I hadn't seen that very often from him. "Tell him that was awkward as hell, but I'm glad." He looked away from James. "And tell him I'm sorry."

"First off, he says that was awkward as hell." James snorted. "He also says that—" I blew out a breath. "He says that he's sorry."

James's hopeful smile crumbled. He ducked his head, hiding the tears I'd seen there just a second ago and pulling his hand away. "He's sorry?"

David had moved back, his eagerness fading. "This was a bad idea."

"Just give him a second." James looked up and scrubbed his eyes with his sleeve, almost knocking his glasses off. I shrugged. "He thinks this was a bad idea."

James let out a choked laugh. "I'm all right." He sniffled and gave me a small smile as he reached for my hand again. How had I gotten so lucky to find someone who could handle that? James glanced toward the back seat. "He's got nothing to be sorry for. It was an accident."

David made a huffing sound. "Stupid accident."

"Right, it was a stupid accident, but no one in this car caused it." How had I become the counselor? I gave all my attention to James. His shoulders were tense; this needed to come to an end. "Maybe this is enough for now."

"Good idea." David leaned forward. "I'm done anyway." The car was suddenly darker without his glow.

"And he's gone. He really is kind of a jerk." James laughed and cranked the car again. It was good to hear, but I had to check. "You need me to drive?"

"Nope." He checked his mirrors before backing out of the space. "Thanks, Nate. For all of that."

"Anytime." I held his eyes with mine. "Seriously, anytime."

* * *

When we returned to my house, James got out of the car and followed me to the door.

"It's a proper date, right?" He was grinning at me, and his face was beautiful in the moonlight. His hand was warm on the back of my neck as he ducked down to press his lips to mine. I put my hands on his waist, under his jacket, and my fingers slid under the hem of his T-shirt, finding smooth, warm skin. It was like a jolt of electricity, and I wanted more of it. My hands found their way up the back of his shirt and splayed on his back. He grinned against my lips.

"It's a little cold out here for that. You want to invite me in?" I smoothed the back of his shirt down but kept my hands under his jacket.

"Maybe." I was feeling brave, so I let myself go for a few minutes. *Just out here making out with my* boyfriend *on the front step. Nothing else to see.* Finally, I broke away. "Okay, definitely." The winter air cooled my heated face as we pressed our foreheads together. Aunt Susan's car was in the driveway, but I didn't think she'd mind. Brave again, I took his hand and pressed a kiss to the back of it before leading him inside.

* * *

"Good date?"

Aunt Susan was, of course, sitting in the living room reading when we came in. She'd deny waiting for us to get back, but I knew better. James found his voice first.

"Yeah, it was fun. We went to that burger place in town."

She nodded and put her e-reader on the side table. "James, can I talk to Nate for a second?"

Uh-oh. I gave him a glance, but he didn't look worried at all, like he'd been expecting her to say that.

He motioned toward the kitchen. "I'll just be in there, okay?"

He was talking to Aunt Susan, and I realized it must have to do with whatever their private conversation had been about. She smiled at him and then waved toward the couch next to her for me to sit. Sitting meant serious conversation. *Great.* I sat.

She waited until James was in the kitchen before beginning.

"Nate—" She looked me directly in the eye, leaning forward slightly. "—is James planning on staying over tonight?"

I nodded, cautiously.

"And where is he planning on sleeping?"

When I blushed, she mercifully didn't make me say it out loud.

"That's what I thought. Okay, ground rules." She held up a finger. "One, he can only stay over on the weekends. That's nothing new." A second finger went up. "Two, let's both agree that I'm not stupid. Take your hands off your face and look at me."

I lowered my hands from where they'd automatically flown and did as I was told.

"Better. Promise me you'll be careful"—my ears burst into flames—"I won't quote statistics at you, but I am a medical professional and know a thing or two. I'm also well aware how grossly inadequate Sex Ed is for straight kids, and it's an utter failure for gay kids. I don't care if it's embarrassing. If you have questions, ask."

Oh my god. I didn't cover my face but clasped my hands under my chin and tried to will her to stop talking.

"Don't look at me like that. I'll pull up freaking pictures that will turn your stomach. Seriously."

"Christ, we haven't—" My face was glowing hotly now, but I managed to go on in a choked voice. "I have the Internet you know."

She arched an eyebrow. "And everything online is true? Never trust porn as your only resource, you're smarter than that, and those guys know what they're doing. You know I won't judge. And if you don't want to talk to me, I can put you in touch with someone you can talk to."

I groaned and covered my face again. "Fine. Okay?" Why were we even talking about that?

She tapped my arm until I lowered my hands and then raised finger number three. "Three, give me a hug, and I'll put you out of your misery." She beamed at me when I lunged forward to hug her tight. "Go on. I'm going to bed."

I escaped to the kitchen to find James perched on the side counter, scrolling through his phone. He looked up, taking in my red face, and laughed. "You survived."

"Mostly." I grinned at him. "She's cool with you staying over, so that's something." A horrible thought occurred to me. "Um, let me go and check my room really quick. Please don't move."

He laughed again and held his phone up, the screen still full of whatever game he'd been playing. I scurried to my room to see if Aunt Susan had left anything in there, trying to be helpful.

Jesus. At least she'd left whatever it was in a plastic bag from the drugstore. I peeked inside and almost swallowed my tongue. Condoms. I looked again. And other things. Thank god I'd come in here first. I tucked the bag into my nightstand and tried very hard to forget it was there. When I turned around, James was leaning in the doorway, grinning.

"Is it safe to come in?"

A strangled sound that might have been a laugh burst out of me. The innuendos were racing through my head. "Very safe."

Our eyes met and the giggles set in. James walked over to me and wrapped an arm around my shoulders, pulling me in close. He kissed my forehead, which was quickly becoming my favorite thing for him to do. It made me feel cherished. Cared for. Yeah. Falling hard, much?

"You mind if I shower?" We'd stopped by his house on the way home, seeing as how he'd come over the night before not knowing what would happen. It was funny how things seemed to work out.

"Go ahead."

He squeezed my shoulders again and grabbed his bag to get ready for bed. We weren't tired, but we'd both earned as much time watching TV in our pj's as we could stand.

As soon as I heard the door of the bathroom close, I went and sat on the side of the bed to wait. Not for James, oh no. For the two ghosts who were absolutely, pardon the pun, dying to talk to me.

"Okay, you two, we've got like ten minutes." I spread my arms out wide. "Let the gloating begin."

"Sweetie, I'm so happy for you!" Nana appeared first, sitting beside me on the bed. If she could have hugged me, she would have. I would have liked that, too. She was beaming at me. "He does seem like a very nice boy, and so handsome."

Oh god. At least Nana approved.

"At least you figured it out." David leaned against the wall next to the door. "Took you long enough."

"Fine. I was wrong. Happy?" Nana gave me a stern look, but I didn't care. I would admit I was wrong, but I didn't have to be gracious about it. I heard the water shut off; we needed to wrap things up. "Okay, he's almost done. Can we talk about this later?"

"Of course, darling." Nana's chilly touch on my shoulder was still odd, but strangely comforting at the same time. "I'm so happy you have someone." She faded away. David was still there, his arms crossed over his chest.

"Take care of each other. I'll leave you to get to it. You're good together." Despite his usual sullenness, I could tell he meant it. He faded as James came out of the bathroom, hair damp and standing up everywhere. I thought so, too.

* * *

The first day back at school was nerve-wracking. Despite the rough start, the weekend overall had been glorious, and I didn't want to get back to the reality of life. The night before, I slept alone and was surprised to find I missed James already. We had swapped positions Saturday night. It turns out sleeping with my nose buried in the hair at the nape of his neck was right up there on my list of "best life experiences."

When James picked me up that morning, I think he could tell how nervous I was. He didn't say anything, just offered his hand palm up in the seat between us. I laced our fingers together and stared out the window. "I don't know what to expect."

"What do you mean?" We were almost to school, and I wanted to beg him to turn the car around so we could avoid whatever hell was waiting for us at that godforsaken place. Even in my head, that sounded dramatic, but a panic attack was coming on at the thought of what Penny Applegate would do if she saw that I was happy.

How could I explain that to James? He knew. I could tell he knew, but I had to say it out loud. "How are we supposed to have this—" I picked up our joined hands "—in there? It's like...like I'm not allowed." I shrugged and looked out the window again. "It's stupid."

He squeezed my hand before releasing it as we came to a halt. He sat there for a moment, not making a move to get out of the car. When he finally spoke, his voice was quiet. "It's not." He unbuckled his seatbelt and turned to face me. "You know these people better than I do, know how they'll react." He picked up my hand again. "I hate how they treat you. I hate how it makes you doubt yourself." He kissed my knuckles, and I had trouble swallowing past the lump in my throat.

"Okay." I nodded and cleared my throat. "Okay." I was so stupidly touched that I found it difficult to form words. I took a deep breath and let it out. And then another. James waited patiently, his hand warm in mine. I looked into his eyes. "Ready?"

He nodded, and I took my hand away to get out of the car, dragging my bag out with me. I shouldered my backpack as if preparing to go into battle. James bumped my shoulder with his to remind me I wasn't alone.

"It'll be fine."

He couldn't promise that. The people here have had years of experience in making things not fine. And coming back late from Christmas break made it worse. I'd missed several days now, not counting the two hours I attempted on Thursday, and that would be remarked upon I was sure. One of the perks of having an aunt who was a nurse was the doctor's note I had tucked into my pocket. Evidently, I'd had the flu and not a mental breakdown. That was encouraging.

I still wasn't sure. "We'll see, I guess." Here we go.

* * *

I made it to lunch without any incidents. That was unusual, even on days when it didn't seem like I had a flashing neon sign over my head that said: "Nate is happy. Feel free to ruin it." People *had* left me alone more since I'd started hanging out with James, but not entirely. Sometimes there was a hard shoulder check when I was walking by myself, or whispers made that weren't completely out of earshot. I tried not to let it bother me, but it wore me down after a while.

It felt like everyone was staring at me as I made my way to our table. They weren't, of course, because I wasn't important enough in the messed up social hierarchy, but it still felt that way. I looked up and saw Margo sitting at the table, *our* table. Why? She was talking to James, but he wasn't looking at her. I was proud of myself for not feeling a rush of jealousy at seeing her there. It might have been different if James obviously didn't want her there.

I sat down with my tray, and James smiled at me across the table. Margo looked at him and faltered, glancing between the two of us.

James spoke first. "Hey."

God. One word, and my cheeks heated. It might have helped if he hadn't looked like he wanted to drag me across the table and kiss the hell out of me. How had this become my life? Not that I was complaining. Really, really not complaining.

"Um, hey."

It was like Margo wasn't there. All I could see were his bright-blue eyes looking at me like that, and I couldn't help the grin I gave him.

Margo snorted. "I *knew* it." She stood and folded her arms across her chest, looking pissed.

Great. Here we go. The day had been going too smoothly. I looked down and pushed my food around on my plate, appetite gone.

"*This* is why you broke up with me?"

James was calm, much calmer than me. "It wasn't the only reason, but yeah. I thought I was pretty clear." Her sharp intake of breath was telling. I had no doubt now that she'd been trying to get back together with him while I'd been out of school. James's voice was chilly. "Oh, and I know you were horrible to him."

Oh god. What was he *doing*? Say something. "No, um, it's okay..." I trailed off at the look on his face. It was a cross between disappointment and sadness that I never wanted to see again.

"It's *not* okay." He didn't look away from me even as Margo stormed off. He sighed softly. "I probably shouldn't have done that, but she drove me crazy last week. Her and Penny." He picked up his fork and pointed it at me. "Do *not* say you're sorry."

The apology had been on the tip of my tongue. I bit it back. "You know she's going to go straight to Penny, right?"

He shoved a bite into his mouth. "Let her." He looked so silly talking around a mouthful of peas that I snickered and rolled my eyes at him. He'd made it better, but I was still worried. I wished I was as confident as James, but then again, I'd had years of experience dealing with that stuff. When he grinned at me, I almost put my hand on the table for him to take. Small steps, small steps.

CHAPTER SEVENTEEN

I had a gut feeling Margo would go to Penny. But it took another two days before she made her move, which meant I spent two days looking over my shoulder and making myself crazy. James was trying to be understanding, but he'd never witnessed the full force of Penny's wrath. Margo was her friend, sort of, and in Penny's eyes, she'd been wronged.

Penny waited until lunchtime on Thursday to strike. Again, what was it about the cafeteria that invited drama? James was running late, so I was alone when she came over to the table.

"Where's your boyfriend?"

Margo was watching us from a few tables away, and I gave her a glare.

"None of your business, Penny. Where's yours?" She was cheating on him with one of the football players, according to everyone, so I might as well make use of that while I could.

"I wonder what he would say if I told him about you? Do you think he'd stick around if I told him that I caught you talking to yourself in the library, and you swore it was a ghost, you *freak*?"

She'd leaned forward, hands flat on the table in an attempt to be menacing, and it suddenly hit me that I just didn't care. The only person I cared about was James, and he already knew everything there was to know. And he cared about and accepted me in spite of it. No, *because* of it.

God, it just didn't matter anymore.

"That's all you've got? Really?" The shock of me talking back was written all over her face. *Good.* I was on a roll. "Guess what, Penny? I don't care."

Over Penny's shoulder, I saw James walk in. When he saw who I was talking to, he picked up his pace, heading for the table. I held up my hand as he approached, and he stopped, watching and waiting to give me backup. And that was all I'd ever needed: someone I could count on to be there no matter what. It had only been a few days, but it was freeing to know that. It was so freeing that I could laugh in her face.

"Go away, Penny. My boyfriend doesn't care about what you have to say, either."

She looked at James, mouth hanging open, as he stood there.

He shrugged. "I really don't." He put his bag down and sat next to me instead of in his usual seat. "Hey."

"Hi." The adrenaline was pumping, so I gave him a quick kiss on the cheek. God, I hoped he was okay with it. He smiled, and I was glad I'd done it. I turned to look at Penny and said something to her I never thought I would: "You can go now."

Red-faced, Penny huffed and turned to stomp off, probably to commiserate with her squad, or look for easier prey.

I was ridiculously proud of myself and a little terrified at the same time. James's smile was so wide he looked a little crazy. I blushed, ducking my head when he threw an arm around my shoulders to pull me in close.

"I am so proud of you." His fierce whisper in my ear was thrilling.

"I can't believe I did that." I was still reeling a little from standing up for myself and from James's reaction.

He gave me another tight one-armed hug before sitting back. "Go get your lunch already."

"Fine, fine. Pizza day. Yum." He made a face, and I laughed.

It hadn't been a week, and I couldn't remember what it was like before James. I didn't want to.

* * *

Afterward, Penny actually gave up. So thrown by my lack of interest in anything she might have to say, she'd moved on to the other little fish at school. As a fellow little fish, I wished them luck.

James was lucky. There were enough people who liked him that he wasn't a target. He had that easy ability to make friends I would never have. I wasn't sure what he saw in me, but I was glad he saw *something*. Okay, enough of that.

* * *

The weekend couldn't come fast enough. It meant James would get to stay over again, and I missed having him in my bed. *Not like that.* Okay, maybe a *little* like that. I hadn't slept well lately. It had taken only two nights for me to become addicted to sleeping pressed up against him all night. God, what would he even think? Clingy much?

We were driving to my house after school, and it was the first time we'd been truly alone since last weekend. And I was freaking myself out. We'd talked a little more about *things* via text during the week because sometimes it was easier that way. There was no pressure, but I'd had absolutely no experience in anything physical, and I was— Oh, the hell with it. I was curious. There, I said it. It wasn't something that had ever been on my radar before. Seriously, why would it have been?

I glanced at him, and he caught me, of course, and grinned.

"Are you panicking again?"

He wasn't making fun of me. We'd already been over that, but I must have been oozing nervousness by now. He offered his hand palm up on the seat between us, a habit now, and I took it, hoping that my own wasn't sweaty. We'd kissed some more, of course—when he was dropping me off, when he picked me up, before we got out of the car at school. Yeah, that was how it was.

I mean, it wasn't like I hadn't looked up *stuff* or anything. I was a seventeen-year-old guy with a laptop and Wi-Fi. Not that I was even thinking of anything like *that*. It was good to start simple. Why was I thinking about this? My face was flushing yet again, and James picked up my hand to press a kiss to the back of it.

"Stop it."

It was like when someone said not to think about elephants, and then that was the only thing the brain latched onto. *Yeah. Elephants. So many elephants.*

"Sorry."

"Nope. No reason to be sorry. I get it." We turned into the driveway, and he shut off the ignition but didn't get out. "I mean, you know I'm not expecting anything, right? Everything is at your pace, whatever you want." He kissed the back of my hand again. "Or don't want." He got out of the car, and I let out a breath. *Elephants.*

I followed him to the door, each of us giving Arthur attention in turn before we went in. Nothing out of the ordinary: Kicked off our shoes inside the door, hung up our coats and headed straight to the pantry and fridge for something to eat, dropped our bags on the kitchen table. Just like always. James reached to get a glass from the cabinet, and I couldn't stop staring at the way his T-shirt clung to his back. The world kept spinning.

* * *

We took our chips and sodas to the living room and sat close together on the couch, shoulders pressed together and elbows knocking as we stole from each other's bowls.

"They were *right there*! If you want salt & vinegar, get your own!" I laughed as he leaned back, trying to hold his bowl out of my reach.

I changed tactics. He barely had time to put the bowl on the coffee table before I kissed him. We hadn't kissed since he'd picked me up earlier, and I got a little carried away. I pulled back, panting, a grin on my face.

"I told you, yours are better." I reached for the bowl to cover my surprise at my own boldness.

"Unfair tactics!" He flopped back on the couch as I crunched on the chips, snickering to myself. He was lying back with his arm flung over his head, and it made his T-shirt ride up. He was beautiful. And he wanted to be with me.

God, I wanted...I wanted to touch that little strip of skin so badly it made me scrub my hands on my jeans. I looked up and realized he was watching me stare at him.

"You okay?" He shifted, tucking his arm behind his head. Watching to see what I'd do. No pressure, no expectation.

I reached out and touched. His stomach twitched under my fingertips, and I smoothed my hand up under the hem of his shirt. His skin was warm and soft, softer than mine. He held out his hand, and I took it, letting him tug me up the couch until we were lying pressed together. I was half on top of him and had no idea where to put any of my limbs.

He laughed softly. "Just relax."

He was so solid and safe that it felt easy and right. My hand was flat on his chest, and I could feel his heart beating under my palm. I looked up. We were nose to nose, so I leaned in and kissed him. It was slow and like drowning in him. His hands were on my back, sparks racing up my spine where they touched my skin. It was overwhelming. And...stimulating.

I pulled back and tried to shift away. "Sorry."

He tightened his hold to gently keep me in place. "Don't. It's fine. Just take a second." He stroked up and down my back and pressed a kiss to my hair. "It's not just you, trust me."

"Oh, I can tell." My voice was muffled from where my face was mashed into his shoulder.

He laughed, was happy and smiling, and I grinned at him. Suddenly I couldn't stand it anymore. I kissed him again, and it all shifted. His hands were up the back of my shirt now. I had no idea how that had happened, but I wanted it to keep happening. I rose up a bit, and he started to drag the shirt over my head when it hit me that we were on the couch in the living room, and it was so not where I wanted to have my first *anything*.

"Wait."

He stopped immediately and pulled my shirt back down. Always careful, always caring. *God.*

"What?"

He was holding perfectly still against me, waiting for me, so I gave him a kiss on the forehead before sliding off him. And promptly fell off the couch onto the floor. He sat up, wincing as he adjusted himself in his jeans, and for some reason that set me off giggling.

He looked down at me, frowning slightly. "Are you okay?"

"Just proving a point, evidently." I scrambled up and held out a hand. He looked at me, confused for a second, before taking it. I tugged him up to me. "That couch is way too small." Confident that it was what I wanted to do, I led him to my bedroom.

"Are you sure?"

"Very sure." I still had him by the hand. "I really think—" That was when a telltale glimmer caught the corner of my eye. *Oh, god.* I stopped so quickly, James ran into me. *Shit, shit, shit.*

"Are you okay?"

I turned to look at James, and though he knew everything, though we'd gone over it, he'd never had to face it.

"Um, there's someone in my room."

He blinked at me and then craned his neck to look past me.

"No, no. There's *someone* in my room." Comprehension dawned on him, and I waited for the rejection. I looked away until he ducked down to look me in the eye.

"It's okay. Do you want to go and take care of it or go back to—" He nodded toward the couch.

I looked through the doorway and could still see the glow of *someone*. I couldn't tell if it was Nana or David, but I was really, *really* hoping it was David.

"Let me take care of this. Okay?"

He nodded, and I gave him a quick kiss before going in my room and closing the door. No reason to expose him to more of the crazy than I had to.

Of course.

Of course, it was Nana. Because that couldn't possibly be any more embarrassing. Christ.

"Hi, Nana." Awkward, awkward, *awkward*.

"Hi, sweetie. How are things?"

Who knew how much ghosts actually saw? Did they only watch us when they manifested, or were they always watching? That was a scary thought.

"Good. Um, can I talk to you about something?"

"Sure. Does it have anything to do with why you closed your door when you came in here?"

God, she was too freaking observant.

I blew out a breath. Might as well get it over with. "Yeah. Um, Nana, I don't really know how to say this but—"

She laughed. "Let me guess. You want me to clear out and leave you two alone?" Okay, that wasn't so bad. "Sweetie, you do have protection, right?" Oh my god. I covered my face with my hands. She chuckled. "I'm sorry. I'll stop."

I peeked at her from between my fingers. "Really?"

"Really." She started to fade away. "I'll talk to you later." And she was gone.

That wasn't so bad. I really needed to lay down some guidelines, though. *God.*

"Okay— Nana, David, and whoever— I'm pretty sure you can hear me, so I just want to say, this room is now a ghost-free zone unless I say so, all right?" I felt stupid standing here talking to myself, but what could I do? I looked around. When nothing happened, all I had to do was open the door and let James in. Just walk over and open the door. Open the door. Door. *Just do it.* I opened the door.

James was standing just a few feet away with his back to me and turned around when he heard the door open. "All good?"

"Yeah." I leaned against the doorframe, suddenly so nervous I couldn't think straight. All I knew was that he was too far away. "Come here."

He closed the distance between us and pulled me to him. Was I shaking? I was shaking. God, why was I so nervous? I was so sure just a few minutes ago and now—

He rested his cheek on top of my head after I pressed my face into his neck. "You don't have to do anything, you know. *We* don't have to do anything."

I moved without thought, my hands coming up to rest on his back, and it brought back that feeling of solidity and comfort. He grounded me in a way I didn't know I'd been missing until he was there. I breathed him in.

"You smell good." I felt his laugh more than heard it. "I didn't mean to say that out loud."

His fingers under my chin urged me to look up at him. He looked amused and fond, and want overtook me again, washing away the nervousness. His lips were soft against mine and, just like that, it felt right again. I slid my hands under the back of his T-shirt, the glide of warm skin under my palms just as good as it was before.

"I can take it off." He murmured it against my lips.

It sounded like the best idea anyone had ever had. I tried to help, and he laughed as he finally tugged the shirt over his head, ruffling his hair even more. His glasses were crooked and his eyes were shining and he wanted me just as much as I wanted him. God, I needed to touch him, to take a moment to just look at him. Running my fingers over the curve of his shoulder and his chest, splaying my hands over his ribs, I couldn't stop touching him. I kissed him, hard, pulled him farther into the room, and closed the door.

* * *

It was a blur of sensation after that. I pulled my shirt off—or he did, I lost track—and it pooled on the floor, and then he was pressed against me. We were lying on the bed. I pulled him down on top of me and my skin was burning everywhere we touched.

He pressed his lips to the line of my jaw. "Is this okay?" All I could do was nod. "Nate, I need you to tell me this is okay." His mouth was on my throat; it was the most okay I'd ever been.

"Yes."

My voice was raspy, and I couldn't think. I wanted him closer, closer, closer. My hands were on his back, clutching at his shoulders. His mouth was on mine, and I was drowning again, his hands in my hair. Our jeans were heavy between us and the pressure was almost too much. I was fairly certain I was about to embarrass myself very quickly. I pulled away from him, gasping. "Hold on."

Our panting breaths filled the silence in the room. I smoothed my hands down his back, and James pressed the side of his face to mine. It was hot and a bit sweaty. I needed to take a breath. "Sorry."

"Don't be. Too fast?" I shook my head because it wasn't. Not really. He pulled away a bit. "Come here." He was rolling off me, and that was so not what I wanted, but he rolled so I was on top of him now. In control. My hips were slotted against his, and he wrapped his arms around me, pressing us together completely. "Better?"

"Yeah."

I leaned down to kiss him as his hands went to my shoulders, my back. Then he slid his hand down until his fingertips were just under the waistband of my jeans. I gasped and moved, knees sliding against the blankets, and he made a noise in the back of his throat that I wanted to hear again. And again. The friction and pressure through heavy denim was too much. I made an embarrassing noise and shuddered, gasping out something, anything, his name, a rush of emotion and pleasure washing over me.

Mortification washed over me for a split second at how quickly it had all happened. But then his hands were on my hips, pulling me down harder against him.

"Kiss me, kiss me." And now *he* was breathless.

I did as he asked as he arched beneath me, gasping into my mouth. Then we were breathing together. He grinned up at me, holding me close and running fingers through my hair. The edge of his glasses pressed into my temple, and I didn't care.

I slid off to the side so I wasn't squashing him, but kept my arm across his waist, pressing close to him with my head on his shoulder. "So."

His chest shook with laughter. "So."

I snorted and buried my face in his neck, giggling until we were both laughing, our skin sticking together and jeans becoming more and more uncomfortable. The laughter finally died away. We held on to one another until James turned so we were pressed chest to chest. He took his glasses off and reached without looking to put them on my nightstand. As he settled back next to me, he dragged his nose across my cheek, his breath making me shiver. Our lips were so close together I felt as well as heard his next words.

"Want to do it again?"

* * *

We ordered pizza and spent the rest of the evening curled up on the couch with a movie that I couldn't even remember the name of. We'd put on pajamas, eventually, and now he was sprawled on top of me, our bodies fitting together like puzzle pieces. I touched him without hesitation now; his hair was soft under my fingers. He sighed and pressed his face into my chest. I liked it—this closeness. Almost as much as— Yeah. *Almost.*

I never wanted to let him go.

"What are you thinking?" His voice startled me out of my thoughts. What could I say to him? I didn't want to ruin everything with my insecurities. He raised his head and looked at me. "Whatever it is, you can tell me."

He said that now.

"I don't— What are we doing here?" He started to sit up, but I tightened my arms around him, keeping him in place. "I'm not saying this very well." I blew out a frustrated breath. "I've never done *this* before, and I'm trying very hard not to scare you away."

"Seriously?" James had gone completely still against me. I was afraid to breathe, afraid that I'd already messed up, and we'd barely started. He looked me in the eye. He didn't look angry, only amused. "Let me see. You love bad horror, will watch comic book movies for *days,* and play vintage video games with me even though you suck at them." He squirmed when I poked him in the side. I wasn't *that* bad. "Do you think talking to ghosts is going to scare me away from that? So what if you don't know what you're doing, no one else does either." He leaned forward, his nose brushing mine. "Besides, I like you a lot. Like, *a lot,* a lot." I was grinning stupidly when he kissed the corner of my mouth.

Couldn't help it. He liked me a lot. He had his own goofy grin. "So, stop worrying. Okay?"

"Okay." I did feel better. But there was something that had been bugging me for days, and I needed to know. "The other day, when I was talking to Penny—"

He laughed. "You mean when you shut her down? Yeah, I remember." He lay his head back down on my chest, still chuckling.

I rolled my eyes even if he couldn't see me. "Yeah, yeah, yeah, I'm amazing. Anyway, I called you my, um, my boyfriend." I pressed my cheek to the top of his head. "Is that okay?"

"Yeah." He tightened his arm around my waist. "Yeah, it is."

CHAPTER EIGHTEEN

School was bad again on Monday. It seemed like the shock had worn off, and people had taken time to think of all sorts of ways to torture me. James didn't get the brunt of it, at least. I had let my guard down. That was my first mistake.

The second was assuming Penny would be the only person I would have to deal with. Margo had been busy over the weekend too. While I'd been getting cozy with my spanking-new boyfriend, she'd been spreading rumors that I had "turned James gay" and stolen him from her. I made it to homeroom before finding that out, despite the usual glares as we walked in. James had to talk with one of his other teachers, so he'd left homeroom early, resting a hand on my shoulder before going. That was when she made her move.

Oh, not Margo, she wasn't brave enough for that. Penny came up to me, sliding into James's seat like she belonged there. I ignored her, giving all of my attention to my calculus notes, until I couldn't stand it anymore. Her eyes were boring a hole in the side of my head.

"*What?*" Rude, yes, but I really, *really* didn't owe her anything.

"Nothing." She shrugged, trying and failing miserably at looking innocent. "Just wondering how a freak like you was able to steal James from Margo. I mean, he certainly wasn't into guys when he was with her." She lowered her eyes, and to anyone else it might look flirtatious, but I could see the real ugliness there. "At least, that's what *she* said. Didn't he tell you?"

Pure, unadulterated evil. Because despite her being full of shit, it still made my stomach clench. It took all my years of practice not to react. Before I could think of actual words, though, the bell rang. She picked up her bag and left me to deal with the carnage she'd left in her wake.

God, I hated her.

* * *

I made it to lunch after enduring stares, giggles, and one hard "accidental" shove that sent me staggering into the lockers. James was already at our table. I could see from the door that he was pissed. His jaw was clenched, and he looked at me as I walked up, his lunch forgotten for now. I took a seat, unsure what to say because I'd frankly had a horrible day and couldn't imagine his had been much better. I just kept it simple. "Hey."

"Hey." He watched as I settled my stuff at the table, trying not to wince when I jostled my bruised shoulder. But he'd seen it. "What happened to you?"

"Nothing." I didn't want to tell him. I so didn't want to tell him, but I was probably going to have to. "It's fine. Don't worry about it."

"Don't worry about it?" He narrowed his eyes, and I really didn't like that look turned my way. "Are you kidding? Was it one of Margo's friends?"

"It's not anything I haven't had to deal with before." I shrugged and winced again. "At least I'm not bleeding this time."

"Not *bleeding*? That's the bar you're setting here?" He huffed out a harsh laugh. "That is so far beyond *not* okay, I can't even—" He stood up so fast his chair skittered backwards. "This bullshit has to stop."

"No, James, wait!"

He ignored me, heading directly for Margo's table, where I could tell the entire group had been watching us. Margo, at least, had the good sense to look worried as Hurricane James headed their way. I was torn between staying where I was, continuing to try to blend in with the scenery so that I didn't get my ass kicked, or following him over there to lend support in his futile attempt for social justice. Yeah, I never said I was smart.

I got over there just in time to hear part of Margo's rant. "—freak like him? Over me?" So we were on to the name-calling already. *Great.* She looked past James at me. "What the hell do you want?" I stopped behind him, at a loss for words. Her face was flushed with rage. "It's not enough that you stole my boyfriend—"

"I was never your boyfriend!" James had evidently had enough. His shout rang out through the cafeteria, mostly because everyone was silently watching the drama unfold. "Oh my god. We dated for, like, a month"—it'd seemed a lot longer than that to me—"and I'm really, really regretting that now." He took a deep breath, trying to calm himself. "So, just stop it. Whatever you're doing, stop it. *Now.*"

"I have no idea what you're talking about."

James's teeth ground together—I could hear them— as he tried not to yell. "You know *exactly* what I'm talking about." Another deep breath. "What are you trying to accomplish here? Do you think if you break us up I'll come running back to you or something?" He leaned forward over the table, looking directly into her eyes. "Because that is never going to happen." Her face paled, and I almost felt bad for her. Almost. Margo was on the fringe of Penny's group and maybe the attention was what she craved, but now she looked like she regretted it. Anyway, James wasn't done. "Say you lied."

I blinked at James. I guess he'd gotten the full story, then. I heard a sniffle and looked over to see Margo's eyes were filled with tears. "James, I—" She took in a shuddering breath. "I'm sorry." She glanced around at the silent table. "I made it all up. I'm sorry." She looked up at James, and he gave her a hard look.

"I'm not the one you should be apologizing to." He held out his hand to me. All eyes were on me now, but I could only see him. I took his hand. "All of you owe him an apology."

I could tell by their faces, a mixture of shame and disdain, that it would be a cold day in hell before that happened, but I appreciated the sentiment.

Margo squeezed her eyes shut and took a deep breath. "Sorry, Nate."

She sounded small and ashamed, and if I were a better person, I would feel worse for her. I only felt *slightly* bad.

James squeezed my hand. Oh, was I was expected to say something? What could I say?

"Thank you." Nana would be proud. It seemed like the entire cafeteria was staring. I was really over it now. I leaned toward James, my voice low. "Are we done here?"

"Almost." James looked around the table, looked at the core group of people that had made my life a living hell for the last five years. "All of you did this. To feel better about yourselves or whatever. All I know is you missed out. You missed out on knowing someone who's funny, and kind, and—" He looked back at me, squeezing my hand. "—the best person I've ever met." He didn't wait for them to respond, just turned away and led me back to our table.

We sat and stared at each for a few seconds before breaking into giggles. He shook with laughter. "Sorry, sorry. I didn't mean to go on like that, and I really didn't mean to make her cry."

I snorted. "You were five seconds away from climbing on the table with a boombox!" That image had us laughing even harder. I wiped the tears from my eyes and smiled at him. It wasn't the last of what we'd have to deal with, but for the moment, it didn't matter. All that mattered was that we wouldn't let them get to us. I wasn't alone in it anymore. I put my hand on the table, palm up, and he covered it with his.

"That was utterly ridiculous"—he ran his fingers over my palm—"and I meant every word I said." He looked at our hands on the table, seemed a little embarrassed.

"I know." As corny as it sounded, I felt like a whole person now. Like I'd finally been found worthy of something special. "You know they're not going to give up, right?"

James shrugged. "Yeah. They're not the first jerks I've dealt with, and they won't be the last. It kind of goes with the territory, you know?" He was playing with my fingers now, and it was sending little tingles of sensation up my arm. Very distracting. "You okay with that?"

"Yeah. I am." I squeezed his fingers, stopping that gentle touch. "I don't have to do it alone anymore." I cleared my throat, trying to break the tension. "We never got lunch." The bell rang, and people around us started to move, dumping their trays and getting ready to go to class. "Damn."

James laughed. "We'll go get pizza after school. How's that sound?"

"Perfect."

* * *

The last few months of the school year flew by. The idiots ran their mouths, and we ignored them. Mostly. There was one incident where a football player ended up with a black eye, but no one saw anything. Funny, how that happens. No one talked about it, and the idiots shut up completely shortly after. Aunt Susan wasn't happy about wrapping up James's hand, but she hugged him so tightly afterward that he didn't know how to react. He looked at me helplessly over the top of her head. All I could do was shrug, though I knew how she felt. I felt the same way. After she finally let him go, she dug a bag of frozen peas out of the freezer, tossed it to me, and left for her room.

It was a long time before she came back out, and then she just hugged him again.

* * *

I finally met James's parents. Deborah and Gary Powell were perfectly nice and not what I was expecting. His mom hugged me when James introduced us. I tried not to be awkward. His dad was a little more reserved, but he shook my hand and had a genuine smile. James looked a lot like him.

Sam, his uncle, was there, of course; it was his house even though sometimes I forgot that part. He gave me a smile and a nod, and again, awkward. I had no clue what had happened between him and Aunt Susan, but they seemed to be friends of a sort. It was none of my business, but Sam seemed to want to get to know me.

"Hey, Nate. How've you been?"

Though I'm pretty sure he meant *How is she?* But I played innocent. "Good. We've been good."

His smile faltered, but he recovered quickly. "Um, I'm headed out. I'll see you later?" He was getting out of there so we could have our "meet the parents" in peace. I didn't blame him. He gave us a wave, and we heard his truck start up a minute later.

James's mom shook her head. "I told him he could stay, but he insisted on 'getting out of our hair.'" She smiled, looking at me curiously. "You've known him for a while, right, Nate?"

"Yes, ma'am. A few years." I wasn't going to give her any info on her brother's love life at the expense of gossiping about Aunt Susan.

She nodded. "That's what I thought. And please, call me Deb. Ma'am makes me feel ancient."

I laughed, and James lost some of the nervous energy that had been coming off him.

I liked her.

* * *

I managed to get through dinner without embarrassing James or myself and counted that as a win. I endured James's teasing about the button-up shirt that Aunt Susan had convinced me to wear because she wanted me to make a good first impression. I guess it worked, because they told me I was welcome anytime and that they'd love to meet Aunt Susan. I had no clue what James, or Sam, told them about her, but they didn't ask any awkward questions about my parents, for which I was thankful. It was comfortable talking to them.

David was there, of course. I excused myself to the bathroom to talk with him because he was getting on my nerves with his lurking around. I leaned against the sink as he paced back and forth in the small space, brushing against me and making the hair stand up on my arms. "They like you, you know."

"Good. Me, too." I kept my voice to a whisper. He paced a few more times and I waited to see what else he had to say.

He stopped and looked me up and down, smirking. "Nice shirt."

I grinned at him. "James told me he likes it. I mean, after he made fun of me for trying too hard."

David made a face. "Anyway. I'm glad they like you because now they won't worry about him as much. He's so much better now and—" He rolled his eyes. "It's mostly because of you."

I flushed the toilet and ran the water to act like I was in here doing normal bathroom things. "You're welcome."

He flipped me off as he faded away.

I found James in the kitchen, waiting for his mom to cut the pie for dessert. I wound an arm around his waist and kissed his cheek without thinking. And then blushed furiously as his mom gave us a grin. "Sorry."

She waved a hand, still smiling as she transferred slices of pie to plates. "It's okay, sweetie. Don't mind me." She stepped over to the sink before continuing, washing her hands. "I haven't seen James this happy in—in a while." She grabbed the towel to dry her hands and held it for a moment before turning toward us. She had tears in her eyes, and James went to her and put his arm around her shoulders.

"Mom, don't." When she hugged him back, it felt like I was intruding. I started to step back but stopped when James caught my eye. He shook his head and motioned behind her back for me to stay. She sniffled and stepped away from him, squeezing his arm.

"Sorry." She dabbed at her eyes with the towel and gave me a watery smile. "Happy tears, I promise. I'm just going to—" She pointed vaguely toward the bathroom. "James, could you put the coffee on, please."

After she left, I looked at James, and he shrugged. "She's still a bit emotional about, um, everything." He grabbed the coffeepot to fill it with water, still talking over his shoulder. "She'll probably cry on you next, so just be prepared."

I leaned on the counter, watching him fix the coffee. "I don't mind." And continued watching as he pushed the button and came to stand in front of me. I gazed up at him. "What?"

He grinned and stepped closer, putting a hand on the back of my neck to pull me in for a kiss.

After a moment, he moved back, pressing his forehead to mine. "Thanks."

"Anytime."

His mom, of course, walked back into the kitchen to finish getting the dessert ready. She smiled at us again.

I pushed James away, a little embarrassed. "Everything okay, Mrs. Powell?"

"Nate, I asked you to call me Deb." She shook her finger at me in mock-sternness and then turned to James. "Is the coffee ready?"

"Almost." James opened a cabinet and started pulling out mugs.

James's dad, who insisted I call him Gary, joined us, and we had our dessert. James had asked if I wanted to stay over, but I felt a little weird about it since I'd *just* met his parents and all.

His mom hugged me as we were leaving, and I thought she was going to cry again, but she held back. "Nate, please come back and see us again soon." She lowered her voice. "We don't mind if you sleep in James's room. He told us you were worried about that."

"*Mom!*" James flushed scarlet, and I laughed.

"Thanks, Mrs.—um—Deb. Maybe next time." She kissed my cheek and finally let me go. Seizing the opportunity, James dragged me out of there before she could say anything else.

CHAPTER NINETEEN

I frowned in the mirror and tried to adjust the damn tie again. Whose freaking idea was it to require ties for graduation? You couldn't even see the stupid thing. Strong hands gripped my shoulders and turned me around.

"You're just making it worse." James pulled the tie off and threw it around his neck, tying it over his own.

"How are you so good at that?"

I was whining, but I'd been fighting with that thing for a half hour. I ducked my head, and he put it back on me, perfectly knotted. His fingers brushed my cheek. Still made my stomach flutter. We'd been together over four months, and that never got old. He kissed the tip of my nose and laughed.

"YouTube and practice." I rolled my eyes and turned to look in the mirror again. He threw his arms around my shoulders and pressed his cheek to mine. "You look good."

I snorted and leaned into him. We were waiting for Aunt Susan to finish getting ready, and then we would all ride to the school together. James's parents were going to meet us there. They were nice enough to let him come over so that we could get ready together.

They were also nice enough to give James a trip to San Diego Comic Con for a graduation gift and included me in on it. It would be our first trip together, and I couldn't wait. We still had to get through graduation first, though.

I looked at our reflection in the mirror again. We *did* look pretty good. "Ready?"

"God, yes. Let's get this over with." He kissed my cheek and spun around to leave the bathroom. "Susan? You ready?"

She was muffled through her bedroom door, but it sounded like a yes.

I followed James into the kitchen to what had become his usual spot—sitting on top of the side counter. Aunt Susan still hadn't shown, so I took the opportunity to slide in between his knees and steal a few kisses until I heard her heels clicking on the tile.

"Do I have to get the hose?" She flicked me on the ear as she walked past us, making me turn around to lean against James's chest as I rubbed at my ear. "So, how do I look?" She spun around and we both whistled.

"Looking good!" James lowered his voice, conspiratorially. "Uncle Sam's going to be there."

She gave us both a dirty look. I'd seen Sam a few times when I'd gone over to James's house, and the last time, he finally asked me about her. She'd blushed so hard when I told her later.

I raised my hands to defend myself. "Hey, I didn't say it." She sniffed and went to finish getting ready.

James pressed a kiss to the back of my neck and then nudged me forward so he could jump down from the countertop.

"You got your robe and stuff?"

He grabbed them off the table. "Right here."

Aunt Susan sailed by, purse in hand, and rattled her keys. "Ready, boys?"

Of course, that was when Nana decided to show up.

"Um, give me a minute?" James and Aunt Susan both looked at me curiously, and I nodded toward the empty corner. "I'll be quick, I promise." It was so nice that neither one of them batted an eye. They both headed out to the car.

Nana smiled at me and waited for them to go before stepping forward and speaking. "I won't keep you. I just wanted to tell you I'm so proud of you, darling." Goosebumps ran up my arm when she held her hand over it. "I worried all the time, but now you seem so happy. Like you've finally found your place."

It was great to finally be seen as not-quite-broken. "Well, thank you for being proud of me, I guess."

"You're about to graduate, darling. What are you going to do after?"

Ah, so that was what it was.

"There are plans being made, don't worry about it. You know, college, that kind of thing." I was glad to be able to reassure her. Come to think of it, I hadn't had a visit from Nana for days now.

James and I had gotten into Ohio State. Now, I just had to figure out how to pay for it. Aunt Susan had offered to help out, but I was trying to do as much on my own as I could. It was going to be a struggle, but it'd be worth it. The housing situation still had to be worked out, but that was another story. If James's parents followed through on the apartment they'd promised, I had a feeling he was going to ask me to stay there with him. The mere thought of it was exciting and terrifying at the same time. We'd both be eighteen and essentially living together. Like grownups. See? Terrifying.

"I'm not worried at all." The hair on the back of my neck stood on end when she put a hand up to my face. "You'll do fine. I'm going to miss you, though. When you go." She took her hand away, and I shifted my shoulders to get rid of the tingle. "I'll talk to you later."

"Love you, Nana."

She started to fade. "You too, sweetie." Gone.

"He's going to ask you, you know." And enter David, stage left. "To live with him, I mean."

"Yeah." David was still a pain in the ass, but we'd learned to tolerate each other. "I want to, but I have to figure out how to pay my way."

"Check out the indie theater near campus. It doesn't pay much, but it'll help." I turned to look at him, and he shrugged. "It's worth a shot. Plus, you know my mom and dad will do whatever they need to, right? To make sure everything works out." He held up a hand. "Just promise you'll think about it, okay?"

"Fine. I'll think about it." It would be a good fit. But I wasn't going to tell him that.

He fidgeted as much as he actually could fidget. "I don't think I'm going to be around much longer."

"What?"

David gave me a wry smile. "Are you kidding me? You've got this. You've both got this." He ducked his head. "James is good, so I think it's about time for both of us to move on."

I hadn't thought of it like that. "He is better. Much better."

"Anyway. I'll talk to you later." He didn't wait for anything else, just winked out of sight, and not with nearly as much style as Nana.

I couldn't contemplate what David had said about not sticking around because now that the kitchen was ghost-free, it was time to go. I walked out on the back porch and watched as James and Aunt Susan sat in the car, laughing about something.

James saw me and waved. "Hurry up, dork!"

I decided right then and there I'd do whatever it took to make it work.

* * *

The ceremony was just like countless other graduation ceremonies across the country. Long and boring. I cheered obnoxiously for James when they called his name, and he did the same for me, with his parents, Sam, and Aunt Susan joining in for both of us. It was kind of great. I found him afterward and wasn't surprised to see him talking to Sarah. They got along great, but I hadn't expected to see her here.

I approached them. "Sarah?"

She turned at her name and threw her arms around me. "Big bro! You did it!"

I hugged her tightly. "What are you doing here? Does Mom know you're here?"

Sarah grinned at me and turned to point. I followed the direction she was indicating and saw my mom at a distance. She was *here*.

James stepped closer and put an arm around my shoulders, tipping his head to rest it against mine. "You okay?"

I was really glad he was there. Mom looked nervous; I could see the flash of gold as she twisted her necklace. "I'm not sure."

Sarah lowered her voice. "Keep an open mind, Nate. She's really trying."

I glanced at Sarah, and she smiled hopefully. I looked past where my mom was waiting and saw Aunt Susan standing with Sam and James's parents. I gave her a wide-eyed look, and she nodded her head at my mom and mouthed, "Go on."

James took my hand, lacing our fingers together. "You want to?"

Sarah put her arm around my waist, on the other side, and I slung an arm around her shoulders. We all walked over to Mom together. Sarah gave me a squeeze and then headed off in Aunt Susan's direction. I was face to face with my mom who I hadn't seen in so long, and I didn't know what to do. I wiped my sweaty face with the polyester nightmare of my sleeve. *Why am I still wearing this stupid thing?*

I cleared my throat, and James squeezed my fingers to remind me he was there. *Deep breath.*

"Hi, um, Mom."

She still seemed nervous but smiled, looking up at me and appearing smaller than I remembered. She fidgeted with her purse, slipping the strap onto her shoulder and then letting it fall to grip at it with her hands. Her hair was longer but still swept back neatly, just as it always had been.

"Nate."

She started to open her arms to hug me and then stopped, as if she wasn't sure it'd be welcome. James moved to let go of my hand, but I gripped his fingers tight, needing him there. Deciding to just go for it, I hugged her with one arm while clutching James's hand. It was all a jumble: I was glad she was here, but angry it'd taken her so long. After we parted, she glanced at James who'd been silent the entire time.

"You must be James. I've heard a lot about you."

When she held out her hand to him, he looked at me, waiting for my nod before shaking it. "It's nice to, um, meet you."

"Who?" I blurted it out awkwardly, and she seemed confused. "I mean, who did you hear a lot from?"

"Oh. It was from Sarah." Of course. I was still gripping James's hand, but he didn't seem to mind. And there was no disapproval on her face when Mom looked at our joined hands. "Nate, I-I know things have been strained for a while now—"

"Strained?" *What the hell?* "You kicked me out." My voice was shaky, and I must have been crushing James's hand by now, but he didn't move.

It gave me a sort of sick pleasure to see her flinch as she gazed at me. The thought made my stomach turn.

"Sorry. That came out wrong." Her voice was so low I could barely hear her.

I wanted to scream at her. *I'm your son. You weren't even invited; why are you here?!* But I didn't. Instead, I stood there waiting for her to say something, anything that would make things better.

"It probably isn't the best time, but I wanted, no, I needed to see you." She smiled a little sadly. "And Sarah convinced me."

Sarah. It would be her idea.

"It's been a long time." I wanted to drag James away from her and never look back. And, inexplicably, I wanted to fling myself into her arms and sob until I was dry.

I didn't do either of those things.

"I just wanted to say that I'm sorry for the way things have worked out. I was frightened—" She stopped and pressed a hand to her mouth, looking at James as if she'd said too much.

Oh.

"He knows." I reveled in the look of surprise on her face. "He doesn't care." James nodded in confirmation, still silent.

So there, I wanted to say. *See? Someone likes me, cares about me, just for being* me.

"I'm happy, Mom. Is that what you wanted to know? Because I am." Frustrated at the tears gathering at the corners of my eyes, I blinked them away. I wasn't crying in front of her. "Aunt Susan has taken very good care of me." I swallowed, blinking again. "You should talk to her, too."

She nodded. "Yes. I will." She wasn't holding back her tears; they were shining in her eyes.

I looked at James, who'd been watching me carefully. "Hey, want to go find your parents?" At his nod, I let go of his hand. I was okay. I needed to do it on my own. "I'll meet up with you in a few minutes, okay?" As he walked slowly away, I could feel his eyes on me, and it helped. I turned back to her. "So."

Mom smiled, wiping her eyes. "You're happy." She made a move to put her hand on my arm but stopped short. "And I'm happy for you. I hope you'll be able to believe that one day."

I ran my hand through my hair. My heart felt like it was going to beat out of my chest. "I don't know what I'm supposed to say to that. I don't—" She looked away, seemed at a loss. I suddenly wanted to make sure she knew how well I was doing. "I'm going to college, you know."

"I know. Sarah told me." I felt the urge to hug Sarah again. Mom was looking at me hopefully. "If you need help, I'd like to— Can I help?"

I wanted to tell her no. That she didn't deserve any credit for what I'd accomplished. But I couldn't. Besides, Aunt Susan couldn't help me with college fees on her own, and I didn't want to take a handout from James's parents either.

"Let me think about it." It was the most I could promise.

"Okay. Can I, um, can we talk later?" She sounded hopeful.

I couldn't decide if I liked that or not. I wasn't trying to be mean, but she had caused so much hurt when I hadn't deserved it. *I can't forgive you right now.* But that might come later.

"Maybe."

She looked resigned, but she seemed to understand. "Okay. It was good seeing you." She was still clutching her purse tightly. "Could you tell Susan something for me?" She rushed on before I could answer. "Tell her thank you and—" I moved without thinking and put a hand on her shoulder.

"She's right over there." I nodded toward where Aunt Susan was waiting (and trying to look like she hadn't been watching us). "I think it would better if you told her yourself."

"I will." She looked up at me. "Can I?" I accepted her hug that time, pulling back after a few seconds. She was still looking at me tearfully when James returned and took my hand again. Somehow, he knew I needed it. She smiled at us. "Take care of each other." And then she was gone into the crowd, heading toward Aunt Susan.

James slipped an arm around my waist, half supporting me. "That could have been worse."

I snorted laughter I didn't really feel, and he held me tighter against him. I wasn't sure whether to cackle at the absurdity of the whole situation, or melt into an emotional mess. It was a relief to lean on James, anyway, to feel his support.

Together, we watched the brief exchange between my mom and Aunt Susan. I could tell Aunt Susan was doing her best to be polite. They didn't hug but gave each other a smile before they parted ways. That was progress. I wasn't the only one who needed to work on forgiveness.

Aunt Susan walked over toward us, a big grin on her face, and gave me a huge hug. "Are you okay?" I nodded against her hair, and she pulled away, still holding on to my arms. "Are you sure?" I gave her a small smile that seemed to satisfy her. "Okay. Good." She suddenly laughed out loud. "You graduated. I can't believe it."

"Gee, thanks a lot." I pretended to be offended, but I saw through her, saw that she was trying to ease the tension my mom had left behind.

She smacked me on the chest. "You know what I mean. You're practically grown up."

"Never."

"That's my boy." She turned to James, who had taken a step back to give us a moment. "Come here, you." She hugged him and said something I couldn't quite hear. They did that sometimes. They probably thought I didn't know they were talking about me. Whatever it was, James nodded and smiled when she went up on her toes to kiss him on the cheek.

She wandered off to find his parents and, more importantly, Sam. We followed along behind, bumping shoulders as we went and sharing a look when we saw Sam bend down to listen to her.

"Hey." James smiled at me, and I couldn't help but grin back. "We survived." He laughed.

"We did."

He looked around at the crowd that was finally starting to dwindle. "Are you going to miss this place?"

I saw Sarah and waved her over. "Oh, hell no." I snorted. "You?"

He stopped and ran a hand down my arm, pulling me to him. "I might miss it a little bit. Some good memories, after all." He leaned down to kiss me. We'd never kissed in full view of anyone at school, so it felt like a statement. A declaration. Whatever. We did it. We'd made it through.

* * *

The next morning, I woke up early despite not setting my alarm and decided to take advantage of the cool morning air. James was still asleep beside me, so I carefully slid out from under his arm and went to pull on my running clothes. I was sitting on the back porch steps putting my sneakers on when I heard the door open behind me. James dropped down beside me, also in running clothes.

"What are you doing?"

He grinned, tying his shoes. "Coming with you."

"Really?" I must have sounded incredulous because he laughed out loud.

"Yeah. Didn't I ever mention I used to run cross-country?"

Just when I thought I knew everything about him, I learned something new.

"Seriously?" I grinned at him as he stood up, looking far more awake than he should.

"Yep. Ready?"

We started down the driveway and quickly made our way, side by side, our shadows stretching out on the road in the early summer sun. I looked over at James, the light glinting off his glasses and shining in his hair. It was perfect; our footsteps, in sync, rang out on the quiet road.

Summer mornings were pretty awesome, too.

About the Author

Jennifer has always been a voracious reader and a well-established geek from an early age. She loves comics, movies, and anything that tells a compelling story.

When not writing, she likes knitting, dissecting/arguing about movies with her husband, and enjoying the general chaos that comes with having kids.

Twitter: https://www.twitter.com/jcozwrites
Website: http://www.jcozwrites.com
Email: jcozwrites@gmail.com

NINESTAR PRESS, LLC

www.ninestarpress.com